FLIGHTS OF FANCY

FLIGHTS OF FANCY

James Allan

Illustrated by Lynn Williams

Airlife
England

This edition published 1989
by Airlife Publishing Ltd.

British Library Cataloguing in Publication Data
Allan, James
    Flights of fancy.
    I.   Title
    823'.914 [F]

    ISBN 1 85310 052 8

Airlife Publishing Ltd.

7 St John's Hill, Shrewsbury, England.

Contents

'Tiger in the Night' and 'They Order This Better in France' were first published in *Pilot*.

'Delayed Arrival' was first published in *Light Aviation*.

'Down in the Glen' was first published in *Aeroplane Monthly*.

Flights of Fancy

Fledgeling pilots often start relating aviation fiction as they describe their first flying lessons to their friends. And it goes on from there, fiction masquerading as fact in hangars and flying clubs, airline crew-rooms and service messes all over the world. Eloquent hands gyrate in the air, illustrating the latest episode of the 'upside down at fifty feet with nothing on the clock' story.

Sometimes the reverse occurs. A completely factual story of the air can be just too fantastic to be taken at face value. In the world of flying the boundary between imagination and veracity is often difficult to define.

Readers of British and European aviation magazines and books are familiar with James Allan's factual writing on technical subjects, navigation and air touring. This collection of short stories gives them the opportunity of getting to know another side of his writing.

In these *Flights of Fancy* he takes readers up with him into the realms of imagination. His stories take us flying over his native Scotland, over Germany and New Zealand, across the Atlantic and the Alps, visiting Vienna and landing at London Airport. But on almost any page we may become aware of a strong ring of truth. Perhaps there are more factual flying stories in this book than first appearances suggest.

Chapter 1
STRING OF PERILS

There are seldom many aircraft around British skies at 3,500 feet. Most commercial and military aircraft fly well above that height; many light aircraft tend to stay lower, keeping clear of airways and of cumulus clouds.

Because of this customary lack of company Paul Lindsay particularly remembered the high-wing monoplane he saw between North Foreland and Calais a couple of years ago, at just 3,500 feet. Kent Radar hadn't warned him of any traffic, but shortly after mid-channel he had seen it, ahead and to his right, cruising at the same level. As Paul's faster aircraft caught up with it, he became pretty certain it was a Cessna 172. Then it changed course, crossed a mile or so in front of him, and soon vanished towards the French coast near Dunkirk.

Paul Lindsay is one of these lucky individuals whose business justifies the operation of a luxurious aircraft, an Aerospatiale TB20 Trinidad, call-sign Golf-Whisky Alpha. A stocky, vigorous man in his thirties, always well dressed, bachelor Paul lives a busy life. His job involves frequent commuting between his company's offices in London, Amsterdam and Dusseldorf and he does this in his aircraft whenever possible.

He was flying again a couple of months later when weather conditions were worse than they had been on that earlier flight. Ostend was reporting three kilometres visibility in rain with broken stratus down to 1,000 feet and Paul was making his way across the Strait of Dover between layers of cloud.

He could see the choppy, cold-looking water most of the time, and at 3,500 feet the visibility wasn't too bad, except while he was ploughing through rain showers.

'There aren't many people mad enough to cross the Channel in a light aircraft on a day like this,' he mused as he switched his VHF set over from 129.45 MHz to 120.6 to advise Ostend he had crossed from London to Brussels Flight Information Region, and to ask for the local weather.

'Roger Ostend,' he had just responded, 'Weather copied. Whisky Alfa, out,' when he spotted the blurred image of another aircraft through the rain-spattered windscreen. This was not a near-miss incident, but it did make Paul start in his seat. The other aircraft was about half-a-mile ahead and to starboard, gradually crossing further starboard. Their relative positions shifted until Paul could lean across the empty passenger seat and look at it more clearly through the drier side-windows of the cockpit. He saw its high wing and fixed undercarriage before it was swallowed up in another rain shower. It looked like a Cessna again, at roughly the same height and nearly the same place as last time.

'Quite a coincidence,' he thought, 'You seldom see any other aircraft when you fly across here, yet that's twice in two trips I've had company. Odd!'

Business kept Paul desk-bound rather than airborne for a while after that. His company, Cherrystone Records, was issuing a series of 'Big Band Sound' LP albums, and he was having to burn the midnight oil. Marketing had to be planned, advertising arranged, artwork approved and text written for the sleeves. Old music it might be, but to sell, it had to be presented just as attractively as new. Paul wrote some of the album texts easily, but others kept him worrying for days. It was difficult to dream up anything about people like Artie Shaw and Glenn Miller that was accurate yet hadn't been used before.

These two albums were still to be finalised when it became urgent to arrange for the German release, so Paul's next trip included a visit to the Dusseldorf office. He had flown to Birmingham the previous day, and decided to route straight across from East Anglia to the Dutch VOR beacon at Haamstede. It feels a long stretch of water in a single-engined plane, but the weather was superb, with clear blue skies above and sparkling green water below. His Trinidad winged Paul across, without so much as a glimpse of any other aircraft on the way.

Ten days later there were problems with the German advertising schedules and Paul had to go back to Dusseldorf from London. It was a hot, hazy, high-humidity summer's day with poor air-to-ground visibility. Paul decided to keep land in sight as much as possible by routeing via the shortest sea crossing.

By the time he left the English coast at Dymchurch he had heard on his VHF radio a Cherokee call mid-channel inbound, while a Rallye and a Bolkow had each left for France several minutes ahead of him, both at 2,500 feet.

Two minutes later the coast of Kent had disappeared in the haze. For the holiday-makers on the beaches below it was a magnificent day but the pilots over the Channel were flying through a disorienting, horizonless void. Paul felt he was poised in a blue-grey sphere of sky, haze and water as he said goodbye to the London controller and made radio contact with Calais.

Whisky Alfa's VOR indicated Boulogne on a 135° course, the altimeter was steady at 3,500 feet and the artificial horizon never wavered. Then suddenly Paul saw an aircraft ahead of him converging rapidly from his right. It was close and as it came even closer Paul banked sharply to the left and dived to pass under it. Frightened and furious he pulled back on to course and watched the other machine dwindle in size as it continued to head east, seemingly oblivious to his presence.

He called Calais again.

'Calais Approach from Golf-Whisky Alfa, I have just had an airmiss about five miles your side of mid-Channel, over.'

'Roger Golf-Whisky Alfa, confirm your present altitude and course' Calais replied.

'Three five zero zero feet on the Channel QNH, course 135 Whisky Alfa.'

'Golf Whisky Alfa from Calais, we have you identified on Radar, but can see no conflicting traffic. Can you give us further details? Over.'

'It was a Cessna,' Paul began, then he hesitated a moment, and his finger came off the transmit button. Calais came back.

'Can you estimate the Cessna's course or give any other details Whisky Alfa?'

'Sorry', Paul replied, 'Negative Cessna. It was a high-winged, single-engined aircraft, fixed gear, type uncertain. Course, easterly, height 3,500 feet.'

'Roger Whisky Alfa, thank you. We're notifying Kent Radar and Le Touquet'.

The adrenalin was still in Paul's bloodstream and his heart was still pumping well above cruising revs, but he was puzzled too. As he flew across Belgium towards Dusseldorf he tried to bring that plane back into his mind's eye. High wing, yes, but Cessna, no. Fixed undercarriage yes, but had it a nose wheel? He couldn't visualise one. It had been close enough to read registration letters yet he'd seen none. Hadn't a clue even what the nationality letter had been. Colour? Well, it had an overall dark paint scheme; not at all like a typical modern light aircraft; in fact, it could have been one of these replicas painted in wartime camouflage.

'Silly B', Paul thought. 'Flying with his bloody eyes shut.'

A few miles and minutes later Paul began to wonder if his imagination had been playing him up. This idea got uppermost in his mind, and, after landing at Dusseldorf, Paul decided to do no more about the matter.

'Apart from making me look a fool, what good would an airmiss report do?' he reasoned to himself, 'I've no idea what the other aircraft was, no identification, no registration. And what's more, the Calais radar operator would swear it wasn't there anyway. What's the point?'

The advertising schedules were sorted out within forty-eight hours and Paul had to get back to London, for his partner Nigel Wotherspoon was leaving for the States to tie up arrangements for the use of Tommy Dorsey, Glenn Miller and Benny Goodman tapes and masters.

Nigel was to be away for almost three weeks. Before leaving he said to Paul:

'If you get a chance while I'm away, see if you can give Helen and the kids a flight in that damned expensive toy of yours. You know how keen they all are on little planes . . . God alone knows why!'

Nigel flew only when it was strictly necessary, and even then tried to ensure there were at least three gas turbines on the aircraft his secretary booked for him. His two young sons must have acquired their enthusiasm for flying from their mother.

For a couple of weeks Paul was too busy in the office to fit in any flying, although his mind did return occasionally to that incident over the Channel. The dark shape of that strange aircraft flashed across his memory quite frequently, and he began to connect that sighting with the other two recent flights when he had been surprised to see aircraft in a normally empty sky.

On the earlier occasions, the aircraft had been too far away for him to see them clearly, but all three had been of a similar high-wing configuration. Or had they? He began to think carefully, to try to conjure up images from his memory.

The last one, he was nearly certain, had been a tail-dragger. The vivid picture he had of it flashing across above his canopy had no nosewheel. The others? He couldn't be sure. But he began to develop the idea that these weren't three chance encounters with three strangers he'd had, but three meetings with the same aircraft.

'I wonder where the bloody thing was, that day I flew from Norwich to Holland', he yawned as he was dropping off to sleep one Saturday night. Suddenly he was wide awake again, as an idea struck him. He got up, stomped across the flat from bedroom to lounge and selected some volumes from his bookcase. He spent an hour flipping through magazines, books on aircraft left over from his 'reggie-spotting' days and even an old copy of 'Janes' he had once bought himself. He was becoming fairly certain that what he had seen hadn't been any of the high-wing machines his books illustrated. It had been a heavier type of aircraft and he remembered an odd bandy-legged look about its undercarriage that nothing here matched.

The nearest approximation he came across was a photo of a Fairchild Argus in an old book of World War II aircraft. But it didn't look quite right. 'Anyway', he muttered to himself, 'What possibility is there of me seeing a thirty-year old communications aircraft over the Channel nowadays?'

Before putting this last book away, he let the pages of photographs flick slowly past his thumb: Airacobra, Liberator, Fortress, Buffalo, Havoc and Maryland, all the vaguely-remembered shapes of American wartime aircraft. Towards the end of the book were some less well-known ones and there, Paul saw his aeroplane. It was unmistakable, from its blunt radial engine to its bandy-legged undercarriage and heavy, stubby-looking fuselage.

It was, of course, utterly impossible. Paul didn't think even the Confederate Air Force would want to preserve a specimen of this ugly old Canadian-built aircraft, the Noorduyn Norseman. But the more he looked the more positive he became that this was the aircraft he had seen. It matched his half-remembered shape better than the Cessnas, Cubs, Citabrias or anything else in his books.

Warming up in bed again Paul was convinced he had identified the near-miss intruder, impossible as it was to believe. But he was more puzzled than ever, for he began to realise the Norseman photo seemed to have the same characteristics as the other two unexpected aircraft he had recently seen. To see a rare bird like the Norseman even once in the eighties would be extraordinary. Three times was inconceivable.

The phone aroused him from his slumber. 'Damn the bloody thing!' he muttered as he lurched from his curtained bedroom through into the sunlit lounge. He picked the instrument up.

'Hello', in one tone of voice, then 'Oh, Helen, it's you' in another. 'Not at all, I should have been up ages ago, but I tend to treat myself to an exemption from alarm clocks on Sunday . . . Honestly, I have been meaning to ring you, but with Nigel away . . . Yes, I agree, it does look ideal flying weather . . . sure . . . okay . . ., then let me see, let's make it 11.30 in the clubhouse, and I'll stand the three of you lunch. And Helen, bring your passport with you. You have got the kids on your one haven't you? . . . Super . . . No, don't be silly, its just as easy to go there as anywhere else, and you can pick up some duty-free Scotch as well . . . Okay, see you there. Bye.'

There was a sudden flurry of activity round the flat as showering, shaving, cornflakes and coffee followed each other in short order. The door slammed as he headed for the garage, flight case in hand. At the airfield the Met Office agreed with Helen's estimate of the weather, and the two children agreed with her on what was a good way to spend a sunny, late-summer day. Paul flight-planned past Southend, down the Thames estuary, and across from North Foreland to Ostend. Nice easy map reading, and plenty to interest the kids. Even over the sea Paul showed them Hovercraft heading for France in a welter of spray, long lazy-looking tankers heading for Europoort from the Gulf, and ferries plying between Zeebrugge and Dover.

It was a superb flight, and after landing, the little group soon found a table in the sunshine on the restaurant terrace overlooking Ostend airfield.

After a leisurely lunch they all agreed that it had been a good outing so far. Paul then suggested a little detour on the way home.

'Let's make it a real international day', he said. 'What d'you say to tea in France before we go home?' The boys chorussed 'Yes, yes, please, let's go to France', and from the look on Helen's face, Paul took it that she acceded too, so he filed a flight plan, VFR via the coast to Le Touquet. Soon they were taxying out to Ostend's 10,000-foot 08 runway.

A 180° left turn after take-off brought the Trinidad over the beaches, and they could see the holiday-makers quite clearly, 1,000 feet below. Paul had decided to make this another sightseeing trip, and headed west along the coast.

Dunkirk soon came in sight; ugly industry, a sprawling town, docks and the big sandy beaches where history was made in 1940.

'It's funny to think that we're up in the same bit of sky where our Spitfires were once trying to shoot down German aircraft bombing our soldiers', said Helen quietly.

'I get that sort of feeling in quite a few bits of sky', responded Paul. 'Over Arnhem or the Ruhr, for example, or Coventry or the Somme.' Then he had to call Calais for clearance through their zone.

'Roger Golf-Whisky Alfa, no known traffic at 1,000 feet. You are clear to route along the coast. Call passing abeam St Ingelvert.'

'Whisky Alfa will call abeam the India November Golf', and Paul tuned in his ADF, listened a moment to the ident, then pointed out the Hoverport and harbour at Calais to his passengers.

After Paul reported abeam the beacon, Calais cleared him to leave their frequency. He switched to Le Touquet Approach on his radio but before contacting them he showed Helen the coastal cliffs near Wissant and Cape Gris Nez.

'That's where William the Conqueror stood and looked across before he invaded England', he told her. 'And Julius Caesar too, about a thousand years earlier.'

'Didn't Hitler and Goering stand there and peer across too?' she asked. 'At least they didn't do any more than peer.'

'Depends on what you mean. The Germans did a lot of damage to England from just down there', Paul told her, pointing to a field above the cliffs, scarred with innumerable hollows under the turf.

'What's that'?'

'A mass of bomb craters and shell holes. We plastered it all through the war trying to get the guns the Germans were using to shell Dover and Folkstone. Then towards the end I believe the whole area was nearly obliterated when we tried to smash up the launching ramps for flying bombs.'

'Ugh', Helen shuddered. 'Even now you can still see the mess it must have been.' She gazed down at the acres of green, pitted with hollows, large and small.

'There's 'nother plane', said one of the children, and Paul looked up quickly. It was over the Channel, well above their 1,000 feet height. Paul watched it as its track brought it closer, and suddenly he felt an icy hand clamp over his heart. It was the Norseman. Again. Paul knew the shape all too well now, and there was no mistake. His mysterious stranger was back.

He couldn't ignore its presence; he had to find out what the hell was going on. He was going to take a closer look.

Whisky Alfa suddenly found itself at climbing power and trimmed back to dispose of the 2,000 feet of altitude that separated Paul from the Norseman.

'It's ah . . . ah . . . an unusual looking aircraft', he said hesitantly, by way of explanation to his passengers. 'I . . . ah . . . I just want to take a better look at it.'

Paul swung the TB 20 up, up and around, approaching the Norseman from behind. As the range closed, he throttled back and positioned his machine a hundred yards from it, level with it, and on its right.

It *was* one of these reproduction wartime aircraft, complete with USAAF decals, camouflage and black and white 'invasion stripes'. Paul edged the Trinidad closer to try to read its registration. But on these machines the letters are often so small one can hardly see them. Paul certainly saw none.

But he did see something else. The fabric of one wing was torn and flapping. There were two large holes in the fuselage. The Norseman weaved to the left then straightened up again, and began to descend. Paul followed it down, but at a more discreet distance in case its pilot decided to veer to the right.

Suddenly Helen said, 'D'you think that chap's all right. He's flying kind of wobbly, isn't he?'

She was right. So were the children when they said they saw some smoke coming from the other plane. There was a streak of oil too, obliterating the paintwork all down the fuselage. Paul suddenly noticed another hole below the cockpit. Had that been there before? And wasn't the tear in the wing fabric getting worse, too?

Paul was on the point of raising a distress call, when the Norseman's nose suddenly reared. It swung starboard, right across Whisky Alfa's path. Paul kicked the rudder hard, pulled the control yoke across to avoid it. He lost sight of it momentarily, then Helen gasped.

'Oh my God, Paul, look!'

Out of her side of the cockpit Paul saw the Norseman in a spin now, a thousand feet below, leaving a spiral wisp of smoke to mark its passage.

Nor was that the only smoke. On the ground behind the cliffs several fires were burning and low scuds of cloud had formed. Instead of the undulating green field there was only churned brown mud, scarred and pockmarked with ugly craters, dotted with twisted piles of blackened girders and shattered blocks of concrete.

Throttled right back, Whisky Alfa followed the Norseman down. Long before Paul's altimeter reached 1000 ft. there was a flash, and black smoke spread above one of the piles of wreckage already there, mingling with the broken low stratus that had appeared over Cape Griz Nez.

Paul pushed the throttle forward and hauled the Trinidad into a near-vertical bank, turning hard to the left to try to see what had happened. With his right hand he reached out to turn up the volume on his VHF set, but got hold of the ADF instead, and, before realising it, tuned it off the St. Ingelvert frequency.

'Damn the thing' he said, peering into the clouds below and getting only glimpses of mud and concrete, twisted beams and lattice girders.

'Damn what thing?' said Helen, almost in a whisper, as she leaned across Paul to see the ground. 'The aeroplane, d'you mean?'

'No, no', replied Paul hastily. 'No, I meant the . . . Oh hell, damn the lot, the radios, the cloud and . . .'

One of the children, who had sat through all the excitement in silence, suddenly asked, 'Where's that music coming from?' and Paul and Helen became aware of the sound of an old swing classic coming from the aircraft's loudspeaker.

'Pennsylvania six-five-oh-oh-oh' sang the close harmony group, and the saxophones and clarinets blended in their orchestral parts. Despite the distortion from the aircraft's audio system, there was no mistaking the Glenn Miller orchestra's hit from the forties.

'It's all right', Paul said. 'I've just knocked one of the radios on to the wrong channel.' He gave up trying to see through the cloud, straightened the Trinidad out of its steep turn and glanced at the ADF. Instead of the correct beacon frequency the digital figures now read 962. Paul let it play on. Helen grabbed his arm and said:

'Paul! D'you realise . . .'

'Yes, by Christ I do', he said. 'I've just begun to realise a hell of a lot.' He told her how he had seen the Norseman before, how he had almost collided with it only a few miles from where they now were, how he had seen it and Calais Radar hadn't.

'I'm not surprised it didn't register on radar, Paul', said Helen. 'Didn't you get the impression it was, well, sort of, what'll I call it, ahh . . . diaphanous?'

'Yes. Kind of translucent. But you saw the holes, and the torn fabric?'

'And the men in it' said Helen softly.

'And the smoke and the oil, too' added one of the children. 'What d'you s'pose they were doing? Making a film d'you think?'

'Yes', said Helen quickly. 'That's probably just what it all was. You are clever to think of that, aren't you?'

'So it really was there', Paul said quietly. 'And yet it wasn't. We all saw it and yet, well . . .'

'Yes Paul, I know what you mean. But let's talk about it on the ground. Where's Le Touquet?'

Paul got his concentration back to piloting. He was about 1,200 feet up, just south of Boulogne. They could see the river beside Le Touquet as the sea sparkled in the afternoon sunshine. He swung Whisky Alfa's nose slightly and looked back along the coast. Not a wisp of that low cloud or smoke in sight.

He switched off the ADF, on which the Glenn Miller number had ended, called Le Touquet, joined, landed and taxied in. The boys went exploring after consuming a couple of cokes. Helen and Paul perched on stools under the aerofoil-shaped canopy above the bar, drinking cognacs.

'I don't normally drink till the plane's away for the night', Paul said, 'but, Christ, I really feel I need it after that lot back there.'

They discussed the whole sequence of events. Paul agreed with Helen that it was the sound of the orchestra that had brought it together in his mind. Never again would he say Glenn Miller simply went missing on a flight from England to France shortly before

Christmas 1944. Paul felt he now knew exactly what had happened. The pilot had climbed above the sleet and low cloud to cruise, between layers, at 3,500 feet. The damage to the Norseman Paul had seen wasn't consistent with the theory that Glenn Miller's plane had been struck by bombs jettisoned from an RAF Lancaster recalled from a raid on Siegen. It must have been spotted by an enemy fighter, which hammered cannon shells into the tube-and-fabric Norseman, damaging its engine, possibly injuring its pilot. Just over the cloud-shrouded cliffs of France, the plane stalled, and spun down through the stratus to crash into the wreckage of a V1 launching ramp that lay pulverised and abandoned in the fields behind Cape Griz Nez.

No one saw it crash that filthy December day. When the fields were later cleared of wartime debris no one had noticed the wreckage of a small aircraft amongst the rest of the shambles.

Paul had a long argument with Nigel over the text for Cherry-stone Records' Glenn Miller album, but Paul was adamant. The final wording must fit what he now knew were the facts.

Occasionally when flying over France, Paul still tunes his ADF to 962 and listens, slightly apprehensively, to that unidentified transmitter. Never again has it played him any Glenn Miller music. Never again has he seen the old Noorduyn Norseman.

One evening last spring, Nigel was puzzled by just how withdrawn Helen was on a visit they had made to Cambridge.

They stopped to see the American military cemetary near there and Helen had noticed, on the wall around the garden of remembrance the name of a certain major in the US Army Air Force Band, one Alton G. Miller from New Jersey. She was remembering that one little bit of World War II that she had lived through, even though she hadn't been born until years after it ended.

Chapter 2
THE COURIER

Most Britons know that the Scottish highlands and the islands off its
west coast are wild and rugged, with scenery and wide-open spaces
the likes of which are hard to find anywhere else in Europe.

The fact that this region also often enjoys days of magnificent,
clear, sunny weather between the regular assaults it suffers from
Atlantic frontal systems, is a better-kept secret.

This secret seems to have been common knowledge for many
years in the world of film directors and producers. Over these years,
many miles of cinema film and video tape have been shot in the area
north of Glasgow and west of Inverness. *Whisky Galore, Laxdale Hall,
When Eight Bells Toll* and *The Thirty-Nine Steps* are just four of the
many famous titles which have used western Scottish scenic
backgrounds.

Years ago the clapper-boards were clacking and the ciné-camera
shutters whirring as another epic was being captured in Technicolor
on the Isle of Mull. Oblivious to all this I was downing a pint of
McEwans in the bar of a small hotel near Glasgow with a fellow
pilot, when the conversation drifted gently from rugby via passing
references to mutual female friends, the weather and the recent

increase to £5 an hour for the local club aircraft, on to a totally new subject.

'The filming out by Calgary Sands is running behind schedule', Douglas informed me.

'What filming?'

'Oh, didn't you know? They're making some spy thriller out there on Mull. Hoped to finish it this week, but they've had some bad luck with the weather and retakes and so on, so they'll be about ten days late in finishing it off.'

'So what?' I said, finishing my pint and nodding to the barmaid to signify I was prepared to foot the bill for the next round. 'So what's all the interest in spy films? I never took you for a cinema buff.'

'I'm not!' Douglas lowered his voice slightly, and added, 'But I've been, well, involved, if you know what I mean.'

'No, I don't know what you mean. And why the conspiratorial whisper anyway?'

'Cheers!' Douglas said, sampling his fresh pint before embarking on a circuitous explanation of what he meant by being 'involved' in the filming activities on the Isle of Mull.

One of the problems about making cinematic masterpieces in such a location, it transpired, was the difficulty and delay inherent in getting the day's exposed film to the processing laboratories in London and hearing the verdict on the 'rushes'. Actors had to be kept at the ready, sets couldn't be demolished in case these rushes were unsatisfactory and the whole scene required reshooting. So Douglas had, as a result of a chance meeting in the bar of the MacDonald Arms in Tobermory, become 'involved'.

His involvement had consisted of violating the terms of his Private Pilots Licence by doing a modicum of flying for hire and reward. It took about forty-five minutes in the club Tripacer to fly to Mull. It took a little skill to land the machine in a flattish field not too far from the golden sands of Calgary bay. It took another forty-five minutes to fly back to Glasgow again, and a minor amount of subterfuge to get the cans of exposed film from plane to car without making it all too conspicuous.

Douglas then proceeded to transfer the cine-film to the care of British European Airways cargo. The film company's representatives collected it from BEA at Heathrow, only a few minutes away from the processing labs, the evening of the day it had been shot. Next day Douglas picked up the processed 'rushes' from BEA at Glasgow and returned them by air to the film director on Mull.

Helicopters were not so common back in the fifties as they are now, nor could keeping one on stand-by for this purpose match the budget of a low-cost production the way Bob's clandestine charter service did.

'Is it worth the risk?' I queried.

'What risk?'

'Losing your PPL, you bloody idiot.'

'They're paying fifty quid a trip', he said quietly.

I deducted the cost of two forty-five minute flights at five pounds per hour from £50 and whistled softly. 'What risk?' I agreed.

'There's just a couple of snags.'

'What?'

'I'm due back at work next week, so I can't do the trips any longer, and the club's taking the Tripacer off line for ten days or so for servicing. Engine top overhaul or something.'

'There's always the Cherokee.'

'It would never get in and out of the only flyable field anywhere near the filming location.'

'Damn.'

'Why the blasphemy? What odds does it make to you?'

'Well, nothing, I suppose, except . . .'

'Except you were thinking you'd be quite prepared to put your licence on the line too, eh?'

'Yes. Suppose I was at that.'

'Well, don't be so bloody straight-laced in future. You sounded quite disapproving a moment or two ago.'

'No disapproval now; just plain downright jealousy.'

It wasn't until long after we had finished our beers and parted company that I suddenly remembered the Jackaroo.

If you don't remember the Jackaroo, then you are lucky. It was an ugly-looking, ugly-flying biplane that looked like a pregnant Tiger Moth. Back in the fifties, when ex-service Tiger Moths were ten-a-penny (or, to be more accurate, round about £100 apiece) someone had conceived the bright idea of converting some of these delightful two-seat tandem, open-cockpit trainers into four-seat touring aircraft with side-by-side passenger seats in an enclosed cabin. The less than elegant result was called the Thruxton Jackaroo. It had two good points. It was, at about £1,500, cheap to buy, if not to run, and it enabled pilots to persuade reluctant female friends to fly with them, absolving the girls from the indignity of cramming their page-boy hair-cuts or Veronica Lake forelocks inside nasty leather helmets.

Otherwise it was singularly lacking in attractive features, but, at least when lightly loaded, it did still preserve most of the Tiger's spritely ability to leap in and out of tiny fields. And I knew a man who kept one in a barn beside some farm cottages near the foot of the Campsie Hills, a mere stone's throw from BEA's cargo terminal at Glasgow Airport. I telephoned him, then telephoned Douglas for details of his contact in the big, bright-lights world of show business. Next day after a couple of check circuits with an apprehensive owner around his field near the Campsies, I was all set to take over Douglas' courier service.

Monday's operation went well. There was a stiff westerly wind that extended the trip to Mull by some ten minutes, but I found the field Douglas had described to me without any trouble. The Jackaroo used less than half its length on landing into the strong breeze blowing in from the direction of Caliath Point.

A mud-spattered jeep with wisps of straw protruding from its tailgate bumped across the grass towards me and a stockily built elderly man emerged from it carrying several large circular metal boxes containing the films.

'Never can trust bloody pilots', was his greeting. 'T'other chap always landed t'other way. Didn't you see me waiting for you at t'other end of the field?'

'Yes, I did see the jeep, but . . .'

'But bugger all! Just bloody awkward, you airmen. Excuses, excuses. Was just the same at Dunkirk. What was your excuse for not being there, eh? Plenty of bloody Messerschmitts there was, but no bloody Spitfires, eh?'

I refrained from telling him I'd been too young even to join the Air Training Corps at the time of Dunkirk. He would obviously have regarded that as just another bloody excuse.

'These are the films for me, I suppose.'

''Course they're the bloody films. You sign for 'em, and get on your way. You're late too, I supose you know. I've been waiting damn near twenty-five minutes for you. Never could trust bloody airmen.'

Douglas had told me the form, so I signed for the films, promised to try to be on time on Tuesday, stowed the load on the rear passenger seats and prepared to depart.

'Bloody funny-looking machine that. Looks even worse than the one t'other chap had. What d'you call it?'

'It's a Jackaroo.'

'Bloody funny name, too. Suits it to a tee.' He turned and headed back towards the jeep. The Jackaroo was in the air long before it had used half the field's length, and the tail-wind helped us back to the field beside the Campsies in just over forty minutes.

For three days the flights went like clockwork. On each of them I brought back with me an envelope containing ten £5 notes as well as the films. The film company was prepared to hand this over only after getting their rushes safely back from London.

Thursday was drizzly and miserable, with cloud-base about 1,200 feet in Glasgow, but the idea of another envelope of fivers waiting for me in Mull spurred me into action. I left earlier than usual, having decided to route across the Clyde estuary, over the Mull of Kintyre and across the sea to Calgary Bay rather than risk going the more direct route via Loch Lomond and Loch Awe. There are too many mountains like Ben Lomond and Ben Cruachan on the shorter route to make it healthy in bad visibility with low cloud around.

The ceiling was down to about 800 feet in Mull, but there was no rain and the visibility was reasonably good. I again found the field easily. But this time when I touched down, the Jackaroo rolled and rolled on and on towards the farther extremity of the field. For the first time, there was practically no wind, and I suddenly realised that the field length was only barely adequate in these conditions. Still, I was safely down, and I knew there certainly wouldn't be any problem about getting off again.

The jeep had a different driver that day, a much younger man in a floral-patterned open-necked shirt and trousers styled more to suit Chelsea than Calgary.

'Where's the old boy?'

'Old Dusty? Busy doing some set-building today. So they sent me to drive his filthy vehicle instead. It pongs, rather.' His delicate nose crinkled disdainfully. 'Smells as though either he or some of his dogs sleep in the thing.' He handed me the films and the all-important envelope.

'Will you be coming to meet me tomorrow, too?'

'Probably.' The young man looked less than entranced at the prospect. 'The final set'll take a couple of days to build, and old Dusty is more useful with hammers and screwdrivers than I am, I suppose.'

'Then maybe you could do something for me.' I told him about the effect of wind on aircraft landing rolls and asked if he'd be prepared to light a little fire of twigs and grass to provide me with a smoke plume to gauge the wind from.

'Sure. No problem', he agreed. 'I'll build it ready and put a match to it when I hear you coming.'

I enjoyed the next couple of days. The weather was behaving itself again, with perfect visibility, blue lochs and ocean, green and grey dappled mountains below, and just the occasional gleaming-white cumulus castle a couple of thousand feet above the old Jackaroo on our daily peregrinations. The young man's smoke indicator worked well, too. I was feeling pleased with life, and by the end of a week I had £300 tucked away beside my flying log book. That represented sixty hours of flying in these days. Maybe I would be able to afford the hours for my commercial licence after all.

Next day, all went well until I reached Calgary. The jeep was there, but no plume of smoke. I circled the field twice. Still no smoke. I decided the young man from the film company must have fallen asleep in the jeep, smell or no smell, so I executed a full throttle beat-up of the vehicle. This produced the stocky figure of Dusty gesticulating angrily beside the jeep, but still no smoke.

I looked around for any other tell-tale wind indications. There were no convenient chimneys in operation. The wave pattern in Loch Tuath, south of Calgary, was a confused mixture of swell and beach-waves running in all directions. There was no tall corn or hay in the fields to show any wave patterns on land either. Cattle are said to stand with their tails to the wind when it is going to rain, but it was obviously set fair, for the Mull cows were grazing at all sorts of odd angles to each other.

I flew slowly across the width of field, trying to decide which way the wind was drifting the Jackaroo, and opted to land towards the west. Over the five-strand wire fence I cut the throttle and pulled back into the three-point attitude, waiting for the rumble of rubber on uneven grass. The Jackaroo floated. I waited. And waited. When the rumble came I pulled back on the stick hard and kicked the rudder-bar from side to side to fishtail the aircraft and get maximum braking effect from the tail skid. This was not one of the de-luxe Jackaroos which had been fitted with wheel-brakes. It had to be stopped in the traditional Tiger Moth manner.

And as I squinted past the engine cowling at the fence at the far end of the field coming closer and closer I realised with relief that the drag from the tail skid was enough. Who needed brakes anyway? The Jackaroo was going to stop with plenty of room to spare.

Just then she did stop. Very suddenly. And with a sickening sound of something crunching and splintering.

I switched off the Gipsy Major, scrambled out of the awkward cockpit and dived under the wing to see what had happened. A large, angular granite boulder that had been lying hidden in the grass had partially flattened the exhaust pipe, torn its way into the belly fabric of the fuselage and ended up by breaking the rear spar of the starboard wing. How it had managed to miss the propeller and undercarriage was a mystery, but for all the good a Jackaroo with a bust wing spar in a remote field on the Island of Mull was, it might as well have smashed the lot.

I stood up again, and felt the breeze on my cheek. A stiff easterly breeze: a tail-wind. No wonder I'd floated into the unknown, untried territory at this corner of the field.

Dusty meandered across the field towards me.

'Had a bloody accident then?' he queried. 'Bloody fliers; all the bloody same. Useless.'

'This would never have happened if you'd lit the fire I asked for', I snapped at him. 'Surely that wasn't too much to ask for!'

'Light fires? In all this?' He gestured at the dry grass and trees. 'Bloody dangerous at this time of year. Everything's like tinder. What d'you want a bloody fire for anyway?'

I started to explain the problem of landing in a short field with an unknown wind direction, but realised I was wasting my breath.

'Hell, Dusty', I said. 'Look at what's happened anyway. What am I going to do for God's sake.'

'Fix it up and get these films back to Glasgow as soon as you can. You've a job to do, remember!'

'God, man, this isn't a bloody bicycle. You can't "Fix it up" just like that. It's no use. She's a goner. It would cost more than she's worth to dismantle her and ship her back to the mainland. What the hell am I going to tell the owner?'

'Let's take a look', said Dusty. He crouched down and squinted at the damage. 'Is that all! That footling little tear and a wee bit of wood splintered? Surely we can fix that here?'

'I told you, it's not that simple. You'd need a new rear spar, then you'd have to dismantle the lower wing, rebuild it, cover it with fabric, dope it, paint it, then find someone able to refit it and rig it. Know anything about flying wires and landing wires, eh? Got a rigger's certificate, have you?'

I had a flash of inspiration. I could tip the Jackaroo up on to its nose, let a bit of fuel trickle out of the tank in the upper wing centre-section, then put a match to it. That way the owner could at least get an insurance total-loss payout.

Then I realised I didn't even know if he carried any hull insurance on the damned aircraft.

Dusty was squatting by the wing leading edge. 'Show me that rear spar you said you needed a new one of.'

I eased to one side the torn fabric on the underside of the wing and pointed it out to him.

'Flimsy little thing like that, and you say it won't fly because just that's got busted? Never did think much of flying machines. Even less now.' He peered at the damage, stroking the stubble on his chin. 'Leave it to me', he suddenly said, getting up to a standing position. 'I'll get it fixed for you. First of all let's get it back off this bloody boulder here.'

We lifted the tail high in the air and the boulder came clear of the airframe. We managed, after a couple of false starts, to push the aircraft a few yards beyond the obstruction, and laid the tail down on a level piece of ground.

Dusty wandered off on his own. I eyed the aircraft carefully. Apart from the obvious mutilation there were no other signs of damage. No nasty, suspicious-looking fabric wrinkles, and no signs of sagging in the damaged wing. Tentatively I tugged at the flying and landing wires. Their tension felt much the same on the damaged side as on the other. But we still needed a new rear spar and a rebuild before the Jackaroo could fly again.

It was then that I noticed Dusty inspecting the fencing around the landing field. He looked at one fence pole, then another, then returned to an earlier one, and with some tools he had retrieved from the jeep, prised the wires free from it, and lugged it bodily out of the ground. Tool-box in one hand, fence post in the other, he ambled back towards the Jackaroo.

'What the hell are you proposing to do with that lot?'

'Fix your bloody aeroplane, of course. What else?'

'You can't fix an aeroplane with a lichen-covered chunk of timber like that.'

'Sound as a drum. Just moss on the surface.' He scraped some of the fungus off with his penknife.

'It's far too heavy.'

He hefted it in one hand, then looked at the Jackaroo. 'Built to carry four, that is. And you're on your bloody own, ain't you? Reckon this and the films weigh a damn sight less than three people, don't you? Here, grab a hold of this, and do something useful instead of just griping.'

He tossed a length of fencing wire in my direction, and bent down under the starboard wing root with his fence stob.

The next half hour is mercifully only a blur in my memory.

'Hold the bloody thing in place, can't you? Twist the wire around that bit of wood there. No, you idiot, not that bit, that one there, for God's sake. Pull it tight. Pull it, I said. All right, all right, I can see it's bending a bit, but it's got a bit more to bend before it'll break. Pull it tight . . . tighter!'

The fence post became strapped alongside the rear spar, a mighty oak reinforcing a spindly sapling. The internals of the airframe creaked and groaned as unexpected stresses in unusual directions caused uncalculated strains within it. Expensive sounds emanated from the delicate innards of the aircraft, then suddenly Dusty rolled out from under the wing, grinning evilly, and pronounced his verdict.

'Better than new, that lot now. Take more than a bloody boulder to break that spar, I'll bet.'

I looked suspiciously at the great chunk of discoloured timber, dwarfing all de Havillands delicate wooden lattice-work. It was totally out of place, totally incongruous, totally unacceptable. And yet . . .

Something had moved in the starboard wing structure as a result of all the twisting and straining that had gone on around the poor rear spar. One landing wire that should have been tight was slack, and one flying wire a fraction too taut.

'What d'you reckon these adjustments are for?' Dusty countered my claim that the Jackaroo was unairworthy with an attack on a turnbuckle, using spanners and a tommy-bar from the jeep's tool-kit. 'No wonder we never saw any of you over Dunkirk if fliers are all as gormless as you seem to be.'

The wires were soon every bit as well-braced as their partners on the other side.

'Don't know what you airmen make all the fuss about. This riggin' business ain't that tricky, is it now?'

I left Dusty to his self-congratulations, and walked twenty paces ahead of the aircraft, turned around and looked critically at its head-on appearance. To my surprise it actually looked symmetrical. Top and bottom planes seemed to form the same pattern port and starboard. The wires on both sides were similar. Even the dihedral angles looked identical.

Slowly I walked back.

'She'll never fly like that. She'll be all out of balance, with that great chunk of timber on the one side there.'

'Maybe it'll help balance out that great chunk of a pilot sitting on the other side,' said Dusty. He had a point, too.

He also had a roll of sticky black insulating tape, and began busying himself with it, patching the torn fabric under the cabin and wing root together, intricately criss-crossing the silver-doped surface with strips of black.

'That'll hold, come hell or high water', he concluded. 'Now all you want's the film canisters and you're off!'

My heart sank. I'd never really believed it would get this far. I was running out of excuses.

Dusty dumped the films on the rear seat in the cabin and handed me the envelope.

'Don't reckon we'll be seeing you back tomorrow', he said, with a knowing grin. 'Unless you can find some other unsuspecting soul to lend you his aeroplane.' I nodded, inwardly praying that there wouldn't be any more forceful reason preventing my return to Mull.

'Filming's nearly over anyway. Reckon we'll manage without you. And your fifty quid for this trip. . . . Well, I'd say that little job I just did on your aeroplane is worth just about that.'

'If it gets me out of here.'

'Don't be so bloody suspicious. It's a wonder the RAF ever got any planes in the air even after Dunkirk if all their pilots were like you. That's a bargain then. Off you go or you'll be missing the London flight out of Glasgow.'

The Gipsy's exhaust found its way out of the distorted pipe, and after an extended run-up I could hear no fabric flapping. Dusty stood grinning widely, and gave the thumbs up. I reluctantly taxied towards the end of the field that I now knew was downwind. I turned to face the breeze, racked my brain for an excuse not to take off that might satisfy even Dusty, but came up with nothing.

So I opened the throttle. The Jackaroo accelerated normally, bumping and bouncing along from one hump to the next hillock. All seemed normal until, as she became airborne, it became obvious that the starboard wing was much more eager to fly than the port. She listed violently to the left, almost digging in a wing-tip. I slammed the stick to the right to correct the bank, and the nose abruptly pointed upwards. I rammed the stick forward into the north-east corner of the cockpit and decided to abandon take-off. Then I saw, at close range, the fence at the end of the field and the tussocky moor beyond, and decided not to abort after all.

The old spring trimmer took some of the strain off my arm in the fore and aft direction on the long, long haul back over Loch na Keal and Lismore, through the Pass of Brander, past Bens Lui, Vorlich and Lomond. But by the time I was over Strathblane and nearly facing the problems of a landing followed by a meeting with the Jackaroo's lord and master, my arms ached from the constant sideways pressure to stop the machine from rolling to the left.

The landing was smoother than I had expected, the reaction of the owner rougher than I'd anticipated. The hull was not insured, so I was glad I had omitted to tell him about my planned conflagration. But eventually the necessary parts were obtained from Thruxton or de Havillands or somewhere and a proper fitter-rigger spent many long and happy hours rectifying Dusty's 'repair'.

I got the bill – a little over £300; just enough to put my lucrative little venture into the red. You can't win them all, but at least I gained a lot of experience and a few illicit hours towards my commercial licence.

I was recounting this story recently at the bar of Glenforsa airfield's hotel in Mull when someone there said he remembered old Dusty.

'Yes', he told me, 'He was a real character that one. Spent most of the war working as an airframe fitter on Tiger Moths at Sywell. Don't think he was anywhere near Dunkirk, though. No nearer than the newsreels he maybe saw at the Regal in Northampton.'

Chapter 3
BLACK KNIGHT IN THE MORNING

Twelve Lycoming cylinders fired smoothly and rhythmically, six on each side of Frank, and two broad-bladed propellors bit into the early morning air, as Genevieve left Kristiansund airfield behind, and slowly lifted her load up towards cruising altitude.

Genevieve carried her name stencilled neatly on her fuselage, just under her left-hand cockpit window. Frank hadn't christened her himself, although she had always been Genevieve to him, his pride and joy ever since he and the finance house between them had bought her. When the authorities in Oslo allocated her a Norwegian registration Frank himself had meticulously painted it on after obliterating the British lettering she'd previously carried, but he had refrained from painting out her name.

She may first have been called Genevieve by her British owner, or perhaps by the Frenchman who'd piloted her before that, or by an even earlier owner in the United States of America.

Genevieve wasn't quite the same age as the veteran car of cinematic fame, but the name seemed to fit the old girl. She was one of the first Aztecs to have followed the Apaches down Piper's production line in Vero Beach, but that was many years ago, years during which Genevieve had worked hard for her living. She still was working hard.

Nav lights glowed against a patch of cloud in the pre-dawn darkness. Frank's feet were cold, and the flight was less than half-an-hour old. He trimmed Genevieve into the straight and level, took his feet off the rudders and stamped them on the cockpit floor to try to restore circulation.

Above the whistle of the airstream around the cockpit and the drum of the engines, his baritone voice began to echo round the bare walls of the aircraft:

'She was a fishmonger, and faith 'tis no wonder,
Her father and mother were fishmongers too'.

Not, as usual, quite in key, and not quite accurate either, although 'Cockles and Mussels' was quite an appropriate ditty for Frank to warble to himself on that trip.

'What a bloody way to earn a living', he sung, to a different tune, and there was a ring of sincerity in his voice this time. He pounded one gloved fist into the other, stamped his feet again, looked longingly at the cabin heat control, and then, for his passengers' sake, resisted the temptation to crack it open, even a little.

Genevieve was the aeronautical equivalent of a tramp steamer. Frank Case, a freelance pilot, lived frugally one month and like a lord the next, on whatever he could earn from flying his beloved Aztec around the skies of Europe. Club instruction, twin conversions, air taxi work, newspaper and film delivery, and in recent years, many lucrative hours associated with North Sea oil filled his log books and helped to reduce his overdraft and pay off the loan against which Genevieve was mortgaged.

It wasn't a bad life . . . at times. Frank shivered again, and tried wiggling his toes inside his leather boots. At least he was his own boss. He blew a breath of warm air down inside each glove in turn, and felt momentarily better.

In the cabin behind him his passengers wriggled and squirmed within their rows of plastic containers, in cold North Sea water to keep them alive and fresh. They were on their way to grace the dinner tables of the swanky restaurants in Brussels, to form part of the Eurocrat executives' expense account luncheons. A load of luscious live lobsters, fresh from the lobster pots in the rocky northern fiords.

This wasn't the most financially rewarding type of flying, but it paid reasonably well, and Frank did this run fairly frequently in the season. The only snags were the ungodly hour of the morning he had to leave Kristiansund and the fact that lobsters die if they get too warm, so the cabin had to remain cold all the way to Belgium.

Frank tried to think of warm things, to keep his mind off frozen fingers. He thought of curry and of gluhwein, of a blazing log fire and of being in bed with Jenny, one of the other loves of his life. (Which did he love the more, he mused. Genevieve or Jenny? Jenny knew bloody well it was Genevieve, and Genevieve didn't really care either way.)

A trace of dawn was beginning to silhouette the mountains over to Frank's left now as he routed south along the coast, but the fiords below were still inky black. Almost imperceptibly the sky lightened, while very perceptibly the numbness worked its way along Frank's limbs. The instrument lights still glowed, and Genevieve rumbled her placid way south. Her passengers intermingled their taped claws and their scaly legs in a constant fruitless search for an escape route from their polyethylene prisons.

Frank looked again to his left. He noticed a light above the jagged outline of the mountain peaks. It was too green to be a star. There was another aircraft over there. He watched as the light grew slowly brighter, and judged that plane to be on a converging course with his. Two or three minutes passed as the other aircraft gradually became distinguishable as a shape behind the light, and when Frank estimated they were about half a mile apart he flashed his cabin lights on and off twice. Almost immediately there was an answering flash of a landing light.

'At least he's seen me', thought Frank, 'and isn't dozing while his autopilot flies itself into me.'

The stranger's course was taking him to pass below Genevieve and, Frank reckoned, a good bit ahead of the Aztec, but, with nothing much else to do, he watched it approach, and suddenly realised it was positioning itself to formate on him.

'Friendly sort of chap. Or maybe he's just feeling cold and lonely like me.'

In the dark all cats are black, and in the pre-dawn twilight all aircraft are that colour, too. As the black shape loomed closer, Frank recognised its outline. A rare bird, these days, and an odd sight to see at this hour and in this place. It was an old Harvard – or Texan or whatever you choose to call it.

'Wonder what the hell he's doing up here at this god-forsaken time of day?'

The Harvard drew up alongside Frank on his left and tucked its blunt wing-tip uncomfortably close behind Genevieve's rounded one.

'Watch it, lad', said Frank to himself. 'That's enough of that. If you come any closer, I'll scream!'

It became a bit lighter and to his considerable surprise Frank saw that it wasn't only in the dark that this cat was black. The Harvard was all one, unblemished shade of matt black, from blunt radial engine to big triangular fin. Even the pilot's head, in its leather helmet, looked black against the slight pinkness of the eastern sky as the sun crept towards the jagged black horizon. Like Frank, he was flying solo.

Frank raised a chilled hand in greeting.

There was no response from the Harvard pilot.

They flew together, parallel with the coast for a few minutes, then the Harvard suddenly banked left, pulled forward a little and repositioned itself slightly ahead of Frank, who now found himself formating on it.

'Thanks, fellow', he mouthed, 'And so long.' Deciding enough was enough he banked right and turned out to sea to put some open sky between himself and his companion.

With his heading about 30° west of the track he had been following, Frank levelled out and looked round hoping to see the Harvard disappear on his left. Instead he found it repositioning itself just inches off his left wing-tip.

'Damn you, you bloody-minded moron', shouted Frank across towards the other pilot. 'I've got more to do than fool around over the North Sea with you.' Angrily he began a tentative turn back on to course. The Harvard let the wing-tips almost touch, but varied its flight path not one degree.

Frank pointed with his right hand to indicate the course back towards the coast that he wanted to take, and the Harvard pilot made, for the first time, an answering gesture. He shook his head, slowly and emphatically, and pointed straight ahead, with the fore-and-aft flat palm movement used in formation flying. That way lay the wide open waters of the North Sea.

Next came another signal from the Harvard pilot. He tapped his helmet earpiece, and then slowly raised one finger, then two, then three, then all five. Momentarily Frank was bewildered, but as the pilot of the black aircraft repeated it, the meaning became clear, and Frank gave him a thumbs-up sign, before tuning his VHF radio on to the frequency of 123.5 MHz.

After a brief interval there was a voice in his headset.

'Frank Case, you bastard; I'm going to kill you.'

The chill in Frank's body wasn't now due solely to the icy cabin temperature. Suddenly he was clammy with sweat, icy sweat.

Frank was no angel, but he'd be the last to admit it. In his up-and-down course through life he'd made a few enemies. He'd always had an eye for a pretty girl, and he'd often been less than scrupulous concerning any other attachments she might have. He'd had to fight for all he'd got in life and he'd stepped on a few toes along the way. And his present line of work wasn't all sweetness and light in its relations with competitors, or at times even with customers.

Frank tried to think who the hell could he have made such an enemy of that he was now the subject of a death threat?

It had to be some crazy practical joke. He pressed his microphone button and said 'What the hell are you talking about?' The slight quaver in his voice rather took the edge off the intended aggressive tone. It made little difference, however, for the only reply was in the same flat, unemotional voice.

'You heard, Mr Case; I'm going to kill you. Pretty soon now. Out', and as Frank looked across to try to recognise the face in the helmet, the Harvard pilot made a further gesture, indicating that the conversation was at an end. He pulled his connector plug out and dangled it against the cockpit window for Frank to see.

This was one situation Frank wasn't going to be able to talk himself out of. He would just have to fly himself out of it. First question: what did the black plane's pilot intend to do? He was heading him out to sea for a start; that much was obvious.

Before Frank could figure out anything further he saw the Harvard inch forward and then suddenly slide across in front of the Aztec. It pulled up abruptly and Frank's left wing dropped like a stone in the turbulence and wing vortices left by the black aircraft. They seemed to thump Genevieve like a giant fist and threatened to roll her over, but Frank wrestled the controls back into position and found himself 500 feet lower, but under control again.

He swung the nose back towards the coast and looked around for his adversary. He'd gone! Frank scanned the sky, moving the Aztec one way then the other to search all the blind spots. The Harvard was nowhere to be seen. He began to relax a fraction, and started to try to puzzle out what was happening to him when Genevieve lurched violently again. This time the right wing swung downwards and the airframe emitted a metallic clang. The Harvard he glimpsed momentarily out of the corner of his eye. It flashed up and behind him, having forced its right wing against the underside of Genevieve's left. It must have been formating behind and below him ever since Frank had recovered last time.

This bump but not only frightened Frank, it spilled some water from his cargo, and put Genevieve into a steep downward spiral, from which he only pulled out at 1,500 feet. The coast had disappeared into the early morning haze. He turned to steer again towards the sunrise, which was his best guide to direction now, with his compass spinning, and gyros toppled.

'One more of these and Genevieve and I are going to be in the bloody ocean', he thought grimly, keeping an eye on the Harvard, above and to his left. As he watched, the Harvard began a dive towards him. Closer and closer it came, looming larger and larger looking blacker and blacker as it approached.

'Christ, this is it!' Frank gasped, instinctively pulling the yoke over and trying to swing away, and so playing the very card his opponent had expected. Just before the apparently imminent impact, the Harvard seemed to broadside itself, its violent sideslip being exaggerated by the relative movements of the aircraft. Turbulence from the squat fuselage hit Genevieve's already lowered wing. Down the wing went and over the top went the Aztec. Frank felt himself lifted against his lap strap, as dust and mud, old screws and crown caps, matches and salt water were intermingled in the cabin air. His stomach hung weightless but tight-muscled within his body. A sudden sideways swing of the fuselage served to crack his skull with a sickening thump against the cockpit roof. Half-dazed he pulled the yoke toward him and felt the g-force press him back into his seat for a second. Then the cabin noise level dropped, and he realised he was about to stall, upside down, a bare thousand feet above the sea. His hands acted instinctively before his addled brains reacted at all. Throttles full, stick back.

'Come round, you beauty, for God's sake, Genevieve, come round', he breathed, as the old airframe eased its nose down, and slowly the speed began to build up while gravity pulled him firmly into his seat. Then too much speed was the problem, with Genevieve's nose pointing directly down towards the leaden waters, as she tried to complete her half loop out of the involuntary roll. Power off, controls back, airframe shuddering, lobster water sloshing around his feet, ocean water getting nearer by the millisecond, and then Frank knew the old girl hadn't let him down. With no more than eighty feet to spare Genevieve was level again, the hungry waves still safely below her oil-streaked fuselage.

Frank resolved not to give the Harvard the chance of another attack from below, so he opened up to full power and dived to wave-top height at full boost. Where in God's name was the coast? They couldn't be that far out, and yet, even with the light mist clearing as the sun rose higher, he could see nothing ahead.

The Harvard was above and well behind him now, but following.

'Surprised to find me still in the sky, I'll bet', thought Frank. He shook his head in an ill-advised effort to clear the stars from his vision. His skull was tender outside but that was nothing to the thumping, throbbing pain on the inside.

He glanced at his watch (Genevieve's dashboard clock had been a joke for many months now) and finally worked out he'd been two hours in the air. No wonder he coldn't see the coast. They must be passing the Skagerrak now, with Stavanger and even the southern tip of Norway behind. So what to do now? Frank was quite sure of one thing. He'd not be safe from this madman until he was on the ground . . . if then.

Should he turn back towards Norway and try to find the military airfield he knew at Lista, or attempt to make it to the field he knew at Kristiansand?

As if reading Frank's mind the black aircraft traded some of its height for speed to place itself between Genevieve and where Frank reckoned the Norwegian coast lay. So Frank swung the Aztec's nose on to a 150° heading, muttering to himself, 'Denmark, here we come.'

His choice was a good one, for the northerly wind had carried him even further south than he'd realised, and the flat, featureless Danish coast came up before the Harvard pilot had a chance to make another move.

Frank felt better with dry land under Genevieve's wings, and edged up to 500 feet to get his bearings. There was more water ahead, then land again, as flat and featureless as the first bit.

'Must be over the fiords west of Aalborg', he surmised.

The Harvard swung across towards him as they passed over a large inland lake. He pulled Genevieve into a harsh rate 4 left turn, braced himself for the slipstream turbulence, and being ready for it this time found himself still well above danger level when he regained full control. His blood pressure was also well above danger level by this time, raised by equal measures of fury and fear.

Suddenly there was an airfield ahead. A fir wood had a rectangular clearing in it with a lake and a minor road alongside a grass strip. The windsock hung limply.

The runway looked a good 600 metres long as it flashed below him. The Harvard was to his right again, so Frank decided on an approach from the east and pulled Genevieve round 270° to curve in to the little runway, selecting wheels down and then full flap as he did. He overshot the non-existent numbers by a good hundred metres, and put on two chilly bootfuls of brake to pull Genevieve up before the end of the damp grass strip.

There's nowhere quite so lonely as a deserted airfield at six o'clock in the morning. After Frank parked in front of the little clubhouse he got out stiffly and a little shakily into the utter silence. The first thing he did was scan the skies for his adversary. There wasn't a sign of an aircraft. He listened carefully. The northerly wind was all but a flat calm here, and apart from the twitter of birds in the woods behind the clubhouse, the only sound he heard was the pink-tink of contracting metal, as Genevieve's Lycomings cooled down after their hard work.

That apart, silence reigned. Unbroken.

The world was all Frank's so far as he could make out. Relieved of the noise and tension at last, his monumental headache began to ease.

The small hangar was empty, the clubhouse was locked, and so were all the windows. It looked a bit run-down, with dusty tables and old notices hanging from their drawing-pins. Some dirty coffee cups gave evidence that someone had once been there, but no one was there now. No one, that was, but Frank. And he wasn't sure quite what he was doing there, or what he was going to do from there on.

The morning sun was begining to warm the air, and slowly the feeling returned to Frank's fingers and his feet. That was pleasant, until he remembered his cargo, and dashed into Genevieve's cabin door to have a look. From the scrabbling sounds, the brutes were still alive, but the cabin was getting warm now, as the sun rose in the blue. None of the containers had shifted from their restraining straps, despite all the violent manoeuvres they'd been through, but all the water had splashed out of them. Deciding that while being warm and dry suited himself, it was decidedly unhealthy for his passengers, Frank grabbed a bucket from beside the hangar and trudged across the little road to the lake beyond it, praying, meantime, that the water would turn out to be salty. He splashed some against his forehead; that helped to clear his brain. Then he tasted a mouthful. It was brackish; better than nothing. For the next half-hour Frank carried cold water to souse each containerful of lobsters with a couple of buckets. That load represented a pretty hefty sum of money. Frank didn't waste money on cargo insurance and this cargo wasn't going to be worth much if it didn't get chilled again soon, and to its destination pretty soon after that.

They must have been on the ground for around an hour, Genevieve and Frank and the thousand-and-one crustaceans, when he looked all round the clear blue sky, listened again carefully, and, having neither sight nor sound of any other aircraft, decided to take off again. The technicality of an illegal landing on a private airstrip in a foreign country he decided could be ignored, since no one, it seemed, had seen him come, nor was likely to see him go again.

Genevieve fired up nicely as usual. Frank took her to the last foot of the little grass field and executed a short field take-off, clearing the conifers comfortably. As he climbed he tried to identify the pattern of land and water under him, and decided finally that he must have saved his skin by spotting the airstrip he so desperately needed somewhere on the south coast of the Danish inland island of Mors.

'Thank God that psychopathic murdering bastard's disappeared', he muttered, as Genevieve climbed back into the cooler air, to the detriment of Frank's personal comfort, but for the sake of his precious cargo. 'Hey-ho, Belgium, here we come.'

He mused over possible complications concerning flight plan timings, radio calls to be made and so on, but decided the incident of the non-customs landing could be covered up easily.

He jumped and his stomach muscles contracted when another aircraft appeared, heading in his direction from over the North Sea. As it approached, however, a butterfly tail and smooth pointed nose proved it to be a Bonanza, which cruised innocently past, a mile and a couple of thousand feet clear of Genevieve.

Frank turned, a trifle reluctantly, away from land, heading west of the Friesian Islands, to cut the corner towards his destination.

'At least in this visibility I'll be able to keep an eye on Heligoland, if nothing else, until the Dutch coast comes up.' He tuned his ADF to 397 to pick up the beacon on Heligoland, then pulled a cigarette from its packet and lit it to try to take his mind off the cold, now seeping again through his hands and feet.

The control yoke leaped out of his numb fingers, his cigarette dropped to the wet floor, and the rudder-bar jarred against his feet. The Aztec reverberated to a metallic clangour, Frank got a glimpse of a huge black radial engine cowling alongside and to his right, just as Genevieve, nose high in the air began to enter a stall turn.

The black Harvard was back. God alone knew where it had been, or how its pilot had located Frank again, but locate him he had, and crept up behind, to slam the Aztec's tail unit with its port wing-tip. Down the black wing must have rolled, solidly against the Aztec's tailplane, swiping the fin and rudder as it passed.

Frank's jarred fingers grappled with the controls, pushing to lower the nose and slamming on full boost to avoid the seemingly inevitable stall. Genevieve shuddered, and recovered her poise just before she began to fall out of the sky. Speed slowly built up again, and as Frank gingerly tried the controls he found he had full rudder movement to the left but it jammed just right of centre. The elevators were free, but didn't feel quite right to him as he moved the yoke gently fore and aft. But they were still flying.

The black plane had climbed high above Genevieve, between it and the coast.

'Why the hell didn't I go the long way round, over land', Frank groaned, watching helplessly as the Harvard seemed to ready itself for a repeat of the dive and skid attack that had almost finished him off further north.

'He'll not catch me a second time', he muttered and as the dive developed, heading steeply towards him, Frank turned directly towards the Harvard, deliberately closing the range. Down came the Harvard, steeper now. Frank began a dive to come even closer under his opponent, forcing him to dive almost vertically. The pilot of the black plane obviously decided enough was enough, rolled 180° and began to pull out ahead of the descending Aztec. Then it seemed to lock into its corkscrew manoeuvre, rolling again, almost getting itself level after the dive, then rolling round once more.

Frank levelled out, low over the waves and watched fascinated as the left aileron of the Harvard broke away from its outboard hinge, flapped viciously in the airstream, then snapped off completely. Simultaneously, the black aircraft rolled again onto its back and dived inverted into the sea. It disappeared in a welter of spray. Frank circled the white patch in the steely blue sea; the disturbed water settled again.

There wasn't even a trace of oil on the surface to mark the spot where the Harvard had crashed. No wreckage, and certainly no sign of life.

'The stupid bastard damaged his own machine more than Genevieve with that swipe!'

Frank straightened out on to course again after a few moments. The nightmare was over, but the identity of the knight in black armour who'd attacked him was still a mystery.

Frank tuned his radio to 133.55 MHz, the Bremen flight information service, in whose region he reckoned he must still be, and put out a 'Mayday'. He reported seeing a single-engined aircraft crash into the sea, and defined the position as a radial and distance from the beacon on Heligoland. No, he wasn't certain of its type, and no, he hadn't seen any registration letters. No again, there was no sign of any survivors, and he had circled low for several minutes.

Bremen eventually transferred him to Amsterdam, and Frank pointed Genevieve in the direction of Ostend once more.

The lobsters were transhipped from Genevieve to a Belgian fish wholesaler's truck a couple of hours later, and Frank looked ruefully at the damaged skin on his fin and the severe dents on the upper surface of his starboard stabiliser. The airflow must have been totally disturbed by the crumples in the metal; no wonder it had felt different.

His first instinct was to start cooking up a phoney insurance claim to cover the cost of repairs. Parked outside in a gale; struck by flying debris. Sounded plausible. They should swallow that one. Ostend is a windy place, after all.

He had to complete a mandatory written accident report on the mysterious crash he had witnessed. When the controller read it, he looked sideways at Frank, his expression showing he thought Frank either drunk or deranged.

'A Harvard?' he queried. 'Are you sure?'
'Looked like one to me.'
'Get a good look at it?'
Frank grunted.
'Yet you didn't see any registration letters?'
Frank shook his head. 'Didn't seem to have any.'
'You may be interested to know that there isn't a single aircraft, Harvard or anything else, reported missing anywhere in Europe this morning. They sent out a chopper to look for your Harvard, and there's a rescue boat out from Heligoland still searching the area.'
'Have they found anything?'
'So far all they've picked up is an aeronautical chart of Denmark with no name on it.' The man's eyes narrowed. 'Don't suppose that could have dropped out of your old Aztec by any chance?'
'Don't you try to come the smart ass with me', Frank snapped, and strode out of the office.

Over a drink in the Ostend terminal Frank thumbed through the wad of notes he'd received for the lobsters. It checked out okay.

He'd made his customary 100 per cent plus profit on that job. He thrust the notes back into an inside pocket of his flying jacket and began planning his next trip.

He called an Antwerp number and arranged to pick up a small brown package to fly up to a wholesale jeweller in Oslo. This line of business was lucrative, but it was only infrequently that he got consignments of diamonds to smuggle. He preferred shifting sparklers around Europe to moving drugs. That paid well, too, but Frank was always more uneasy when he had hard stuff on board. Too risky. And his occasional contacts among the grass and coke pushers didn't always seem as trustworthy as his clients in the jewel trade.

Next he needed a legitimate cargo to camouflage his diamond run to Oslo. He called Rudi, one of his usual contacts in Belgium. It was his pretty, little, dark-haired Flemish wife who answered. Rudi was out of town till the end of the week. But Frank didn't waste the phone call. He managed to talk himself into company for the evening and a cosy bed for the night.

He fixed a return load of electronic parts next morning. He also straightened the twisted parts of Genevieve's empennage sufficiently, he reckoned, to get him safely back to base. And by late afternoon he was cruising at Flight Level 70, comfortably warm with the cabin heating on, tunelessly singing to himself those words he could remember of 'Diamonds are a Girl's Best Friend'.

It took the accident investigators several days to analyse Genevieve's wreckage, strewn half-across the side of a mountain to the west of Gardemoen airfield. They finally reported the cause of the crash as being a mid-air collision with an unidentified aircraft. This they deduced from what they termed 'pre-crash structural distortion of the airframe' and from several strange scrapes and flecks of black paint adhering to parts of Genevieve's wreckage.

Perhaps it was Frank's botched-up repair of the tail-unit that let him down. Then again, perhaps it was just that whoever had taken out a contract on Frank Case's life, wasn't the sort of person who gave up easily.

Chapter 4
PAT

The first time George Frame met Pat he was quite convinced she was a boy. She and her parents had drifted down one Sunday to the 'wrong' side of the airport away from the jet-whine, the rubber flooring, chromium-plate and PA announcements of the terminal building. They had been watching several brightly coloured little aircraft flying around and Pat's father had decided that sunny autumn afternoon to try to find out where they came from.

He succeeded in locating a wooden hut beside a run-down looking hangar which served as the terrestial quarters of the Paragon Flying Club. Parked between the hangar and the hut were three light aircraft, tiny and fragile-looking in their gaudy red and white paint schemes.

Out of curiosity he accompanied Pat across the grass towards the little planes. Pat's mother stayed in the car. George watched them from the club hut window as they approached the Cessna nearest them.

'Scuse me, Sir' he called through the open window, 'But we don't like kids touching the aircraft. Can I help you in any way?'

'Well, we're really just looking around. I'll see Pat doesn't do more than look.' He ruffled the blonde hair with his hand, and Pat left it ruffled. 'What kind of a plane is this anyway?' he asked.

George removed himself from the window, sighed and crossed towards the door of the hut with a resigned shrug of his shoulders. He grinned in the direction of the other club members.

'My day for the PR work is it?'

His baggy denims and slightly grubby T-shirt proclaiming 'Pilots Prefer Banking to Insurance' were in sharp contrast to the other man's Sunday-best blazer and slacks. The slogan on George's chest puzzled Pat's father, whose business was closely involved with insurance, but he refrained from making any enquiry about it.

'Pat's always been keen on planes' he explained, almost apologetically using the child as an excuse for his presence. 'Keeps watching them flying over the house, and prattling about learning to fly. Wants to be a transatlantic jet pilot or something . . . don't you!' He ruffled the blonde hair again. 'Ridiculous ideas kids get at the age of nine.'

'No reason why Pat shouldn't get to be an airline captain, with a bit of luck,' volunteered George, smiling to the child.

'And a bit of money too, I'd reckon.'

'Some youngsters are lucky and get sponsored training'.

'Mmmm' came the less-than-enthusiastic reply.

Pat remained silent, gazing at the flimsy-looking two-seater with its wing apparently perched precariously on top of its transparent cockpit windows. She found her tongue, and asked in an awed whisper, 'Can you fly that one, mister?'

'Just landed it a few minutes ago,' said George.

'He would be the man flying it while you were watching from the other side of the airfield probably, Pat.'

'Coo.'

There was a look of hero-worship in the deep-violet eyes as they widened despite the glare of the sun.

'Want to sit inside it, Pat?' asked George.

'Can I, really? But the man in there said not to touch it.'

'That was me.'

'Then it's okay?'

''Course it is. Come on, I'll help you up.'

While Pat tentatively wiggled the control yoke and tried in vain to make her plimsol-clad feet touch the rudder pedals, her Dad was asking George about a pleasure flight.

'Can't really do it, 'cos I've only got a private licence,' explained George. 'But if you'd like to call it a trial flying lesson, then you can pay the Club for it and I'll give you a quick trip.'

Pat was bubbling over with excitement. Her father put on a show of bravado, trying unsuccessfully to cover up his nervousness. Her mother flatly refused to go. Then she decided that she wasn't going to be left alone in the world after the inevitable fatal crash. She came but made no attempt to disguise the fact that she was as nervous as a kitten.

George saw Pat and her mother safely strapped into the rear seat of the Paragon Flying Club's Cessna 172, and explained to his third passenger the desirability of keeping his hands and feet clear of the controls. Then he taxied out, did the checks and they trundled gently into the air.

'Bit different from a charter Boeing to Mallorca isn't it?' George called over his shoulder towards his back-seat passengers.

'I wouldn't know about that', came the answer, rather primly, from Pat's mother. 'I've never been up in any of these things before.'

Pat herself merely asked, 'Please, mister, can I undo the strap now and kneel up and see out of the window better?' to which course of action George agreed.

A wide, sweeping, extended circuit of the hills and fields and little towns around the airfield occupied about twenty minutes, after which George asked Pat to sit down and strap in again, before he returned his passengers safely to *terra firma* once more.

Beside the hangar it seemed very quiet in the sunshine after the propeller jerked to a stop. The adult passengers thanked him, then clambered out cautiously. Pat scrambled to follow them. George pinched the tightly stretched denim over Pat's bottom and said, 'Hey, son, didn't you enjoy it then?'

'Course I did, mister. It was super. Honest! Could do it again and again and again all afternoon.'

'No you couldn't', interjected her father, 'We're not made of money.'

'Pity,' said Pat, turning to look at George again 'And don't you call me "son" mister. I'm a girl, see!' She tossed her head, flicking her hair into place, and stared him, almost defiantly, straight in the eyes.

George looked again at the deep-violet of the eyes, and realised that despite the unisex sneakers, jeans and sweat-shirt he should have realised at first glance that no boy could ever have eyes quite like these.

George always got a kick out of introducing youngsters to the joys of flying in light aircraft. The pleasure of seeing nerves relax and tensions evaporate as the fledgelings began to take an interest in their new environment was always something he enjoyed. Their reactions were as varied as the kid's sizes, shapes, sex and sensitivity. The dinky-toy traffic fascinated some, the unknown colours of the hills from above attracted others. A few barely glanced at the world outside the cockpit, seemingly mesmerised by the instruments, but most junior passengers could be relied upon to become ecstatic if you got them into close proximity of a cumulus cloud.

Some became queasy at the slightest bump or the miniscule increase in 'g' of a rate-one turn; others, frequently the girls, squealed with delight at the unaccustomed sensations of a really steep turn or an undulating switchback flight.

It was fun getting youngsters to share his own delight in flying, answering their questions, listening to their ingenuous comments, seeing the light in their eyes as they told their friends on the ground all about it after landing. To George, a pleasure shared in that way was a pleasure more than doubled.

He frequently fondly imagined that his having given these young passengers a first taste of flying, might encourage at least some of them to develop their own interest in it. In fact he seldom saw any of them a second time. However, in Pat's case it was the sparkle in her eyes that he best remembered about six weeks later when she turned up at the Paragon Club hut one afternoon on her bicycle and peered on tip-toe into the window. He recognised the pools of violet below the fringe of blonde hair immediately.

'Hi Pat! What are you doing back here?' he called. 'D'you want to come in?'

The eyes flickered round the room, taking in the other club members present. 'No, mister, you come out please' she asked him. He joined her outside.

'What can I do for you, then?'

'I want another flight please, mister' came the unambiguous reply.

George explained the problems about money, and insurance and the need for parental permission as best he could to a child of nine.

He was better at explaining the effects of controls or the formation of carburettor ice.

Pat kicked softly at the rim of her cycle wheel, and studied the resulting mark on her polished sandals, eyes downcast, as he talked. George finished his explanation.

'You mean no?' she asked, looking wistful.

'Fraid so.'

There was a pause, silent but for the putter of a Cessna on the approach, then she said,

'See my bike's nice and shiny?'

'Sure is!'

'Did it myself. Washed and polished it this morning.'

'Good for you.'

'I'll make your aeroplane nice and shiny too.' She nodded in the direction of the Cessna. 'I'll be ever so careful.'

'It would take you a lot longer than a morning to do that, Pat' George smiled.

'I don't care how long it would take.' The wistfulness had gone. Her eyes flashed determination now. 'I'll wash it and wash it and polish it and polish it till it's like new 'gain, even if it takes ever so long. Honest. It needs it, too', she added, pouting her lips and glancing at the muddy wheel-spats and rain-streaked fuselage flanks.

'Why do you want to do all that, Pat?'

'So as you'll take me flying 'gain.'

'Look, I'm sorry I can't do it for you today, but maybe I'll try to arrange something one of these days. Have you got a phone at home?'

'Course we have.'

She gave him the number, stayed to watch the aircraft for an hour or so, renewed her offer to wash and polish the Cessna, then departed with her brown sandals, white socks and blue jeans vanishing in a blurr as she pedalled her low-geared bike furiously home.

George discovered her family name was Stanmore, and discussed the situation with Pat's father, who eventually, after long deliberation with his reluctant wife, gave George permission to take Pat up occasionally.

'Don't let her make a nuisance of herself, though', added Mr Stanmore. 'And above all, don't be going running up bills for flying, please.'

'No, no, don't worry', George assured him. 'She'll just get the odd trip when there's a spare seat in the aircraft, and won't be in anybody's way. And I'm going to accept her offer to clean the planes, from time to time too.'

'That's a good idea, Mr Frame. You'll soon sicken her of aeroplanes that way, if my experience of getting her to help wash the car is any guide.'

Mr Stanmore was wrong. Over the next few months members of the Paragon Flying Club gradually became accustomed to flying gleaming clean Cessnas, with spotless windscreens.

The sight of a little blonde girl stretching and rubbing with bucket, sponge and chamois, or polish-tin and yellow duster became a familiar one around the Paragon hangar for the next year or two.

And Pat flew. Front seat occasionally, rear seat more often. She flew not only with George, but certainly most often with him.

Then she fell in love. Not with an aeroplane. Certainly not with George. With Roger. Roger was a skewbald horse, and Pat found, like so many girls before her, the ultimate in teenage fulfilment in learning to control and to care for her new-found passion. For the next two years she spent all her spare time around the stables.

George grew a little older, and despite his business commitments, managed to keep on flying. His business, which involved selling fertilizers and foodstuffs to farmers, was prospering, and despite his flying he became a little wealthier. He found his savings at one stage were sufficient to pay for an instructor's rating course, and a year or so later, to put down an adequately large deposit to become the proud owner, in conjunction with a finance company, of his very own aircraft. It wasn't particularly shiny, and it certainly wasn't new, but it was his. Registered in his own name. 'G-AVKV-Piper PA28 Cherokee 140-George Frame' the list of registrations read.

Kilo Victor had been George's for only a couple of months when one Saturday afternoon he decided to try to make his pride and joy a little more worthy of pride by washing at least some of the mud off it. Awkwardly balanced on one bent knee and one straight arm he was busy trying to remove some stubborn grease from the fuselage underside when he became aware of a new feature just inside his peripheral field of vision. Or to be more accurate, two new features, mirror images of each other. They were long, slender, well-proportioned nylon-clad female legs, visible, from his vantage point below the wing, from the smart-looking, medium-heeled shoes that supported them to well above the knees.

George craned his neck round to get a better view. A female voice from somewhere out of sight above the wing said 'Needing any help down there, mister?'

A small bell rang in George's memory. He wiggled backwards from under the flaps, and straightened his stiff back awkwardly. It couldn't be. But the violet eyes had remained unchanged during Pat's metamorphosis from tomboy schoolgirl to sophisticated sixteen-year old. There was no doubt in George's mind as to who the unexpected young lady visitor might be.

She duly admired his new acquisition, and accepted eagerly his offer of a demonstration flight in Kilo Victor.

'No need to ask if your feet can reach the rudder pedals now', said George as Pat wriggled into the front passenger seat beside him, her short skirt emphasizing the length of her legs. 'This trip you can really get a feel for the aircraft, if you haven't forgotten all I ever taught you.'

She hadn't. Nor had she forgotten how to look like a tomboy in denims, as she proved next morning when George arrived at the Club around eleven o'clock to find his Cherokee looking smarter than he had ever seen it look before. Pat's blonde hair was bobbing up and down, in and out of sight on the far side of the tail-fin, as she polished silicone-wax vigorously on to the starboard tail-plane.

'Hey, you're a fast worker, young lass', he called to her.

'Not really. I've been at this since about half past seven', she laughed. 'You should be ashamed of yourself, letting it get so filthy and lying abed on a Sunday instead of helping!'

'You shouldn't have done all that yourself, Pat.'

'I enjoyed it. Honest! I've got used to getting up at the crack of dawn on Sundays to brush and comb these stupid horses down at the stables, and now I can't break the habit. Must say Kilo Victor looks far better after the treatment than Roger ever did, though.'

'Maybe the stables never let Roger get as dirty as I've let poor Kilo Victor.'

'Mmm. P'raps you're right at that too.'

Pat had a well-earned back seat flight that day while George dinned the rudiments of circuit flying in to one of his pupils and in the evening, after his instructional duties were over for the day he

said: 'How would you like a front seat trip before we put Kilo Victor
to bed for the night?'

'You don't need to, really,'

'But I want to. You've earned it. C'mon.'

They taxied out and took off. George handed over control to Pat
at 1,000 feet above the hills south of the airfield and left her to her
own devices. The Cherokee curved gently to the right, straightened,
curved left, then right again, a little more steeply this time. The ball
on the slip gauge stayed strictly central. Pat's touch on the controls
was delicate, balanced and smooth.

'Oops, sorry', she said suddenly.

'Sorry about what?' George was puzzled. She touched the
altimeter with a slender index finger.

'I've lost nearly a hundred and fifty feet. May I put on a touch of
power for the next turn?'

'My God, Pat, if I can get most of my pupils to hold their height
that closely after their third lesson, I reckon they're doing well. And
I mean in straight and level, never mind medium turns.'

She followed him through, her delicate hands poised lightly on
the controls, as he brought the aircraft downwind, across the base-
leg then into finals and the round-out to a smooth landing in the
calm evening air.

'That was a beauty', she said admiringly. 'Just the way I'm going
to be able to do it one day.'

'You'd rather learn to fly than go in for show-jumping?'

'Pooh! That's kids' stuff. I'd like to be an airline pilot, if I could
only afford it.'

'I doubt if you've much chance of doing that.'

'Why not?' she said spiritedly. 'You once said there was no reason
why I couldn't. Very first time I flew with you. I've never forgotten.'

'But that was . . . ah, well, to be honest, when I said that I really
thought you were a boy . . . you know, Pat, Patrick . . .' he ended
lamely. Her eyes flashed defiantly.

'I don't see what difference that should make', she asserted 'I'm
seventeen next month, and I'm going to try to get my pilot's licence.
I've got a bit saved up, I'm not wasting any more money on horses,
and if you'll let me help you, cleaning and keeping your books and
so on, maybe you could, well . . . I'm not looking for any favours,
but I thought . . . maybe?'

The violet eyes were wistful again.

'We'll see', said George.

And they saw.

Pat tended the telephones and hammered the telex machine in a local timber wholesalers during working hours. In her free time she spent all she had saved on learning to fly. George made a present to her of a half-inch thick blue-covered log-book and neatly inscribed on its flyleaf in his best copperplate writing, 'Patricia Stanmore'. He lent her his own dog-eared copies of Birch and Bramson's textbooks on flying. She soloed after six and a half hours of George's instruction and they celebrated the event in the clubhouse bar, with Coca Cola for Pat and Double Diamond for George. He thought he'd never seen a young girl look quite so lovely; she was still up on cloud nine with elation, and the sheer exuberance and satisfaction at her achievement positively glowed from those radiant violet eyes.

George reluctantly charged her normal club rates for the hours flown in his aircraft, but he flatly refused to accept a penny from her for his instruction.

'Let that be our little secret, he told her. 'Quid pro quo for all the elbow-grease you've expended over the years in keeping the planes presentable.'

'Presentable? You've got a bloody cheek George! They're the best-looking club planes in the country, I'll bet.'

Twenty minutes out from base one autumn afternoon on the first leg of a cross-country exercise, Pat stiffened in the seat of the Cherokee, when the engine note suddenly died without warning. It took her about three seconds flat to raise the aircraft's nose, to check the engine instruments and fuel gauges and then to realise George had pulled the throttle shut while she was looking for her first turning point.

'Simulated engine failure', he announced. 'Whatcha gonna do?'

Pat put textbook theory into airborne practice, did her checks methodically, made her dummy 'Mayday' call and selected a field for the forced landing.

'Give the engine a quick burst of power every 500 feet or so', George told her, 'Just to keep it from getting too cold. Which field are you aiming for?'

Pat did as he told her, and pointed out a long, level-looking meadow with a few trees down one side and a road running near it.

'That's about the best one, I think', she said quietly concentrating on positioning Kilo Victor for a safe glide approach.

'I thought you'd pick that one', said George. 'You're right; it's dead into wind, clear of obstructions, pretty large and smooth looking . . . and it's close to the road. Watch your airspeed now . . . don't try to stretch the glide . . . you're doing nicely!'

'Shouldn't we overshoot from here?' queried Pat as the altimeter crept down past the 600 feet mark, her hand ready on the closed throttle.

'Don't really need to. Carry on your approach and see how you do. We're not coming within 500 feet of any persons, animals or buildings here, and I don't see any vehicles on the road either.'

A few seconds later he added 'Right Pat, that was super; you were overshooting slightly, but could have got in beautifully. I have control now.'

Kilo Victor's engine came smoothly back to life, and they accelerated level with the tree tops as the meadow flashed past a few feet below them. Over the upwind hedge George banked the aircraft to the left away from the road and a nearby farm house, then followed a stream towards a small lake, still just hedge-hopping. He banked the other way and circled tightly round over the lake. Pat felt as though the starboard wing tip below her was about to touch the water surface at any moment. Then back they went, faster and faster with the wind behind them, over the stream, across the hedges, past the trees again then suddenly, with a burst to full throttle, George eased the nose up, and Kilo Victor surged up into its own element once more, carrying two exhilarated pilots with it, after this taste of the thrills of low flying.

'Your first turning point is coming up, two miles . . . ahead now, Pat. Restart your timings from there, and if the engine fails again this trip, it'll be for real. I'm not springing any more spoofs on you today.'

'You can do that to me any time you like, George. That was *the* most thrilling bit of flying I've ever done, back down there.'

'Concentrate, girl! You're 15° off course. We'll talk about that once we've landed.'

That evening he told her how he often used that field for forced and precautionary landing practice. It was well clear of any houses, set in a tract of arable land where the farmers seldom put any animals. He knew the local farmers through business anyway, and they knew him and his aircraft well enough not to complain even if he did sometimes come a fraction closer than the legal 500 feet from their houses. In short, it was one of those rare areas where it was possible to fly well below 500 feet without breaking any of the rules of the air.

'But don't let me catch you doing that sort of thing solo, my lass. Not before I've given you a full briefing on low flying, anyway. The optical illusions that the wind can cause near the ground have been enough to kill many a pilot and I don't want that happening to any pupil of mine. Not even to you!'

Pat listened and obeyed. She flew, and learned, passed her written examinations and her medical, flew her triangular solo cross-country and found her general handling test little more than an interesting exercise flown with a different instructor. She had her licence.

Even her mother plucked up enough courage one day next spring to fly passenger with Pat as pilot. Life was sweet.

She still flew with George frequently. As her hours built up he flew with her, usually in Kilo Victor, but sometimes in the club's 150 Aerobat, to teach her the techniques of looping and rolling, stall turns and rolls off the top. Aerobatics terrified her at first, and at the same time fascinated her. Gradually she mastered all that the Aerobat was capable of performing.

They flew together through the silky darkness of velvet summer nights, under skies speckled with countless pin-prick stars and across enchanted fairyland scenes of earth, all its ugliness obscured and reduced to necklaces, chains and skeins of amber, white and blue lights. Pat added a night rating to her licence. Then an IMC. Then she started working for her own instructor's rating, promising herself that once she got it she'd say goodbye to telexes and telephones and try to earn her living from circuits and bumps instead, until that commercial licence was within her reach.

She invited several members of the Paragon Flying Club to her twenty-first birthday party, held in the small functions suit of the hotel between the airfield and the town. Not unnaturally, George was one of the several. Pat had discovered that there are more palatable drinks in the world than Coca Cola, and towards the end of the evening she found herself dancing with George in something of a haze, while the disco operator played one of his rarer slow numbers. George felt her body melting and merging gently with his own. Her perfume tantalized his nose; her hair touched softly on his cheek. He found himself talking quietly to that wisp of blonde hair.

'Pat, I know I shouldn't be saying this. I'm a good ten years older than you are, but I've . . .'

The soft, yielding body suddenly stiffened and the out-of-focus strands of hair were replaced by a very sharply focused pair of serious violet eyes.

'Please, please, George Frame, don't spoil it all.'

He opened his mouth to say something, but she raised two slender fingers and pressed them across his lips. 'Don't say anything else, for God's sake. I know you're fond of me. You don't need words to tell me that. I'm fond of you too. In fact, I think I'm in love with you. Have been for years. But I've got another love too. A demanding, damned expensive love. And that one's got priority. Got me hooked.'

They continued to move slowly in time to the music. Their bodies were slightly apart now, but their eyes locked and their minds in tune. Pat continued softly: 'Maybe we could make it work, despite the ten years. They don't matter. Not really. But it couldn't work while I'm still in love with flying. George, you're a dear, but you're slightly squiffy and so am I. And I'm going to be an airline pilot, remember, George, not a suburban housewife.'

Her fingers gently left his lips, but their eyes didn't leave each other's. She gently placed her lips in the place her fingers had just vacated. Then 'The Girl from Ipenima' was replaced by a flurry of Tamla Motown and their kiss ended. Neither of them broached the subject again.

Kilo Victor's engine was running out of hours. George's business had been running into recession and his bank account was running out of pounds. It looked as though the Cherokee would have to feature in one of the small ads at the back of *Flight International* until Pat announced one day that she'd had a talk with her Dad, and he'd given her enough to pay for the engine rebuild and to buy a half-share in Kilo Victor. She told George how the conversation had gone.

'Flying seems to be the only thing you're interested in', her father had said finally. 'And since the money'll be coming to you one of these days, anyway, I suppose you might as well have the use of it now.'

So George and Pat became partners. Each paid a share of the running costs and insurance *pro rata* to the hours they flew. Pat instructed on Kilo Victor during the week. George flew it at weekends. And occasionally they still made a flight in it together, just for the joy of flying.

Pat taught her own pupils forced landing practice, often using the same field south of the hills, which George had introduced her to, and occasionally gratifying her own urge for the thrill of low flying in the same area.

She flew some football-fan friends of her father's to Monchen Gladbach, to let them see Borussia play their local team. She competed in the Jersey rally one year, did only reasonably well, but enjoyed it hugely. The next year one of the wealthier club members asked her to fly with him in the Malta rally. Her horizons broadened. Places like Le Touquet and La Rochelle, Karlsruhe and Copenhagen, which had never meant any more to anyone in the Stanmore family than names in geography books, gradually became familiar to her. She met and became friendly with Germans and Belgians, wealthy owners of business twins and penniless pilots trying, like herself, to build up careers in the only world they loved.

And she did love this world she'd chosen. She loved the etherial beauty of a cumulus top at close quarters and got more pure satisfaction out of a perfectly judged landing in a twenty-knot crosswind than many people get out of a whole lifetime. She enjoyed passing on her own delight in flying to friends, passengers and pupils, and she began to appreciate what it was that had inspired George to help her convert her childish dream into an adult reality.

Meantime competition continued to make inroads into George's business. Life became tough. He found at the end of its third year that he couldn't afford his usual change of car, even for a smaller model. Flying became a luxury he could only afford if someone else, in the form of a pupil, was footing the bill. It was getting near the stage where he'd have to think about selling his part-share in the Cherokee. Would Pat and he be able to find someone else to take it over? Could Pat maybe persuade her dad to put up some more capital to let her become sole owner? Or would they both require to sell, so depriving Pat of the one and only ladder she had available, up which to climb towards her cherished CPL goal?

George worried about what to do about his animal foodstuffs and his agricultural fertilizers. He worried about what to do about the Kilo Victor and about Pat, and about the battery and clutch he needed for his car.

On his way home one drizzly October evening he made a final call on his friend who farmed near his favourite forced landing field. Driving past he was vaguely aware of something different, but it didn't really register with him what he was seeing. Slightly cheered up by a bigger than expected order at the farm, he only realised what the change was as he drove back past the field again. Running at right-angles to the road and the row of trees, and sweeping right across the middle of the field was a line of high-tension electricity cables slung from aluminium-painted lattice pylons more than twice the height of the trees.

'Damn the Electricity Board', thought George to himself as he drove past the new giants striding across the pleasant landscape. 'I'll have to look for another good field for forced landing practice, if I do go on flying. This isn't a very healthy place any more.'

He didn't see Pat that week, and at the weekend the weather was so squally that only one of George's Sunday pupils turned up. After the lesson George decided to try to cheer himself up by making one short, solo pleasure trip, and having a look at the pylons from the air. As he'd expected, they were all but invisible in the poor light under the overcast, and as he'd feared, they made his favourite field too dangerous to use. He swung Kilo Victor round low over the lake and began to climb to clear the cables and then the hills on his way back to the airfield. It was then he remembered that Pat had got into the habit of using the same field for the same purpose.

'I'll phone her tonight', he promised himself. And he tried. But there was no answer. And by Monday it was potash and fertilizers that filled his thoughts rather than pylons and flying.

It rained off and on most of Monday and Pat lost several instructional hours. But by Tuesday the depression had dragged its way across the country and the weather was fine for flying. She spent most of the day in the circuit. Only one of her pupils was at the stage where she could climb high above the hills and watch his apprehensive face as she persuaded the reluctant Kilo Victor into a spin and recovery.

After her final pupil there was still an hour of daylight left. Pat decided to use a little of it to feel the plane respond to her own touch instead of her pupil's. She climbed above the airfield and headed south. The hills were aglow with the crimson and orange reflections of the sunset. Autumn-tinted trees looked almost like tiny flames, far below. The lake in the plain beyond seemed, from 2000 feet, to be a pool of molten metal. On an impulse Pat completed a meticulous figure of eight with an exuberant wing-over and, with throttle and carburetter air controls both pulled fully back, she pointed Kilo Victor's spinner towards the fiery glow of the little lake. She gave the engine a couple of bursts of power to keep it warm in the chill autumn evening air, and pulled out of the dive a couple of hundred feet above the water.

Then she followed the path she'd followed a dozen times before, along the stream, towards the meadow. The long shadows seemed to emphasize the thrilling feeling of speed at low level. The autumn leaves on the row of trees were a kaleidoscope of russet-browns and yellows and brilliant oranges. The wispy cirrus on the far horizon had turned an unreal pink, and against the pink was silhouetted a strange spider's web lattice . . . God! . . . an electricity pylon!

Instinctively she opened the throttle and began to pull back on the yoke to climb. Then she saw the wires, hanging in the air before her in four parallel sweeping curves, just too high for Kilo Victor to get above them. She pressed the yoke forward again, and time seemed to stand still as the aircraft responded, gently nodding its nose towards the grass meadow. Its inertia carried it inexorably up towards the wires. They seemed to drift forward towards Pat, growing from gossamer-thin threads into solid-looking hawsers. Then the elevators began to take effect and the menacing cables eased themselves out of Kilo Victor's way. Pat's heart leaped with relief. She was about to pull back to avoid hitting the grass of the meadow when the lowest of the cables contacted the VHF aerial just above the cockpit. The world disappeared in a blinding blue flash and a viciously violent jerk as the cable hooked itself into Kilo Victor's tail-fin, severed it, and tore the rudder from the fuselage.

Blinded and stunned by the 100,000 volt flash Pat was mercifully unaware of how Kilo Victor's nose reared skywards, then dropped as the tailless aircraft swooped towards the meadow. The propellor tips sliced a series of slashes into the turf, each longer than the last, as the sculptured shapes of the blades were buckled and awkwardly twisted forwards. The nose cut into the soft grass and ploughed an ever-deepening furrow of brown soil across the meadow. Juddering, the aircraft decelerated. The maimed tail swung itself sideways. One wing tore itself asunder. Kilo Victor came to rest, inverted, half buried in a stack of dried hay.

The unholy shriek of tortured, rending metal ceased. The silence that replaced it was broken only by the ticking of the hot engine contracting, and the gentle trickling sound of petrol escaping from ruptured tanks.

Then came the initially soft sound of a muffled explosion. The fuel ignited, and soon the crackle and roar of all-consuming flames filled the air.

By the time the fire-brigade reached the scene, there was little for them to do, but damp down smouldering hay and look aghast at a blackened aero-engine, blobs of melted aluminium, a mutilated propellor and the few steel fittings that were all that had survived the intense heat.

Pat's parents decided not to go through the sham of burying a weighted coffin containing what might have been some ashes from their daughter's body. There was instead a small service of remembrance. Members of the Stanmore family sat near the front of the chapel and preserved a studied coolness towards the handful of flying club members near the rear of the little congregation. As he formally shook hands with Mr Stanmore on his way out of the chapel, George wanted to blurt out, 'It was all my fault. I should have warned her. I knew the wires were there.'

But he stayed silent, burying his guilt with his grief.

It was when I met George and Pat Frame at Waitaroa airfield in New Zealand that I heard the whole story of Kilo Victor's end. As the starboard wing ripped off the fuselage, it split the cabin apart and threw the unconscious Pat clear.

She had come to, lying in the undergrowth near a beech tree. The firemen were coiling up their hoses, stamping out the last glowing embers in the grass, and preparing to leave the scene. Befuddled and in a state of shock, she watched them go, watched the darkness steal over the scene, watched the harvest moon, huge and yellow, rise behind the autumn leaves.

As she started to shiver, she pulled herself together and began to think, quickly, concisely. Cautiously, she struggled to her feet. Her shoulder ached, her temple was grazed, her sleeve was torn, but there seemed to be no bones broken. Slowly she hobbled across to the remains of the aircraft. Scarcely anything was recognisable, apart from the engine, but in the moonlight she saw blackened pieces of metal from the instrument panel, safety-belt clips, screws, a door lock. Her half-formed thoughts began to take over.

Deliberately she pulled the metal buckles off her shoes, took her wrist watch off and held each for a full minute in the flames of her gas lighter. Then she dropped the buckles, blackened and discoloured, the watch with its strap and face burned away, into the ashes beside the skeleton of Kilo Victor. And she walked off, into the night.

In London she met two Australian girls working their way round Europe, and went with them for a while. In Istanbul she joined forces with an Israeli and a New Zealand girl. She travelled with the latter all the way to her home in South Island.

It was from there that she wrote to George. She asked his forgiveness, and implored his silence, to avoid further grief for her family and to prevent complications concerning aircraft and life insurance policy payments that had been made. And finally she declared she had feigned death to help him, because her love for him was deeper than for anyone else in the world.

George left his moribund business in England and came to New Zealand with all that was left of his capital from Kilo Victor's insurance. He used it to make a new start in business there. Now he not only sells fertilizers to the farmers all around Waitaroa, he applies it too, from the air, in Pawnees and Fletchers.

They have been married for several years, and their neighbours know them as a happy and contented couple. But over a beer in the local hotel one night George confided in me of his ever-present feeling of guilt about Pat's parents. And one lunchtime, while George was off top-dressing paddocks from the air, Pat told me about her constantly recurring nightmare. She has always kept it secret from George. It is about a crop-spraying aircraft, high-tension cables, a violent crash and fire.

And in the nightmares, the pilot never gets thrown clear.

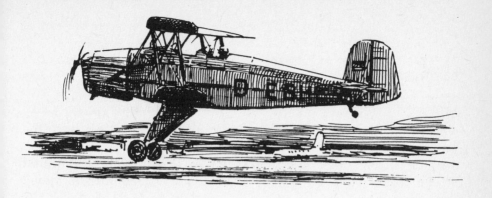

Chapter 5
NIGHT FLIGHT TO TRIER

There seemed to be a tension in the ebony blackness of the sky above the aircraft. A three-quarter moon hung like a yellow lantern almost level with my left shoulder. In every direction the multitude of pin-pricks of light that are our visible evidence of other worlds sparkled against their jet black backcloth.

The instruments glowed their reassuring readings from the panel and above my head the outside air temperature gauge was just visible in the combined red reflections of the cockpit light and pale diffused moonlight. Vibrations running through the airframe were causing the thermometer needle to resonate, almost as though it, too, was shivering in the minus 9°C cold.

I had taken off from Wels in Austria as the winter sun was setting, tinting the snowy Alps with pink and turning the lenticular clouds high above them into rolls of orange and red candy-floss against the blue. I skirted along the Czech border, following the Danube past Linz and Passau. The last traces of cloud had disappeared by the time the lights of Nuremburg city appeared 6,500 feet below on the port bow, and night had taken over from the evening twilight.

This was genuine VFR at night. The visibility was unlimited in all

directions, including up. East of Frankfurt's busy airspace I watched
Wurzburg drift past directly below, then saw Giessen and Marburg
ahead. Fulda's lights twinkled away over to starboard, near the East
German border.

Above, the stars gleamed even brighter in the winter sky. The
cold began to get to my feet through the aluminium skin of the
aircraft's floor. I again began to get the feeling of tension. I sensed
this blackness above and around me shrinking in the cold of night,
stretching itself tighter and tighter across the heavens, just as
though, if it got any colder, it might rip and tear asunder, along the
fragile line of the Milky Way.

The cockpit heating was on full, my hands and body snug
enough, but below my knees I was slowly becoming numb. I moved
my feet from the rudder pedals, stamped them on the cockpit floor
and massaged each calf in turn, to try to warm them up a little. I
checked the instruments again, including the OAT. It had gone
down to minus 11°C. I checked the Milky Way again but it still
didn't appear to have developed even a hair-line crack.

Flying north from the Siegerland NDB I was making the transition
from radio navigation to mixed map reading and dead reckoning.
Even a setting moon shows up the surface of a lake at night as a
distinct light patch against the dark background surrounding it. I
was now looking ahead, as did some famous British pilots nearly
half a century ago, to catch a glimpse of the moonlight reflected
from the waters of the Moehne Dam. The first gleam of water that I
saw was the wrong shape, and came up five minutes too soon. That
was the Henne, not the Moehne lake. Then, right on cue, the silvery
surface of the vast reservoir slid into view beyond its surrounding
forest-shrouded hills. Only another five minutes to my overnight
stop now. I again drummed my soles on the floor and rubbed my
legs to restore the feeling in them, ready to enter the Arnsberg
circuit and land. Due west along the long length of the Moehne
lake, across the sharp cut-off of the massive dam wall, and 270° for
another four minutes and, yes, there were the runway lights of
Arnsberg.

I'd chosen this airfield for two reasons. There is a good restaurant
and a comfortable little hotel on the airfield, and I was too tired to fly
on to my Antwerp destination that night.

As I turned off the tarmac of the runway, the grass sparkled white
in the beam of my landing light. The air temperature outside was

still minus 9°C. I would have a lot of ice to scrape off the aircraft before I took off in the morning, unless I could find a corner of the hangar for her. But the hangars were full, and locked for the night, so I resigned myself to a de-icing job after breakfast.

The little motel-type bedroom in the airfield hotel was none too warm. I just dumped my flight case and overnight bag, freshened up a little and wandered back into the snug warmth of the restaurant overlooking the icy, moonlit airfield. I was surprised to see the silhouette of another newly arrived aircraft parked alongside mine on the tarmac. You don't expect many aircraft movements so late on a bitterly cold December evening. I was even more astounded when I recognised the black outline of the aircraft against the frosty background. It was a Bücker Jungmann biplane. Who on earth, I wondered as I ordered myself a schnapps and studied the menu, had the stamina to endure the open cockpit of a macho aeroplane like that on a perishing night like this?

The Bücker's nav lights snapped off and I saw the figure of the pilot heave out of the cockpit and jump down on the far side of the aircraft. Just as I ordered a large beer to keep my schnapps company, the door of the restaurant opened and in came a gust of icy air and a pilot, dressed in leather boots, a fur-collared, heavy, grey flying suit, leather gauntlets and a helmet. The goggles were pushed up on to the helmet, and it was a very young-looking face that smiled towards me from its frame of grey fur and brown leather.

'Damn cold night for an open cockpit', I said.

'Certainly is; but you can keep surprisingly warm if you dress properly.' The voice was light, and melodic in tone.

'It's warm enough in here at any rate. Care to join me?'

'Delighted to. Just let me pull off some of this clobber. That your aeroplane outside?'

The leather gauntlets were discarded, then the helmet. I watched in amazement as a slender girl, blonde hair plaited into pigtails and tightly wound around her head in an old-fashioned Germanic style, unzipped her flying suit and emerged like a butterfly from its chrysalis, in a pale blue lambswool sweater and slightly crushed white jeans. She put both hands to her hair and eased it slightly from her scalp to loosen it.

'Excuse the hair style', she said, 'I hate it like this, but it's the only way I can fit it into the helmet.'

She seated herself opposite me, a truly beautiful girl in her early twenties, blue eyes sparkling and face aglow from the stimulation of the flight and the chill of the night.

'Can I offer you a drink?'

'Just an Apollinaris, please.'

I ordered her mineral water and watched her study the menu, wondering idly what that remarkable face would look like, framed in free-falling blonde tresses instead of its present severely coiffured setting.

Her long delicate fingers pulled a cigarette from a Camel pack and she lit it with an expensive-looking silver lighter. She blew a plume of smoke gently towards the lamp above the table. I caught myself visualising that face and the long golden hair freed of its formal plaiting, against the pillow in the room along the corridor.

With an effort I pushed the thought below the surface . . . at least for the moment. We chatted on about food, about flying and other innocent subjects.

I had assumed, perhaps wishfully, that Renata (we were soon on first-name terms) was overnighting at Arnsberg, as I was.

I tried to persuade her to have an Asbach brandy with her coffee but she insisted she never drank before flying. It was only then I realised I wasn't going to have her company for much longer.

'You can't go off again into that arctic night.'

'I've got to. Honestly.'

'There's surely nothing so important that it couldn't wait until tomorrow.'

'Yes, there really is. You've no idea how much I have to get done, and how little time there's left.'

'Such as?'

'I've got to get to Trier tonight where my future father-in-law is meeting me at nine. We go straight to the woman who's making my wedding dress, for a final fitting. Then tomorrow there's the rehearsal at the church and so on and on. I don't want to bore you with the details. I'm getting married in Trittenheim on Saturday.'

I don't know quite what expressions may have transitted my face as I digested this news and my subconscious readjusted itself to cancel all ideas of what might have been that night. Renata interrupted these thought processes again.

'D'you happen to have a landing chart for Trier?' she asked. 'I've stupidly come away without one and although I've been there often enough with my fiancé, it's the first time I've flown in solo after sunset.'

I walked the few paces along to my room, collected my Bottlang Flight manual, looked briefly at the white pillow that would never now feel that blonde hair flowing over it, and went back to Renata. The slacks and sweater were already disappearing under the heavy green gaberdine material. I found the Trier airfield pages, unclipped the ring binder and extracted them.

'That should do you', I suggested. 'If you really have to go. It's the best I've got anyway.'

'That's super', she said. 'Don't suppose I'll need them, but better safe than sorry. Tell you what. Scribble your name and address in the margin, and I'll mail them back to you tomorrow. Keep your manual complete.'

'Okay.'

As I scribbled and Renata tugged at zips and thrust her feet into boots, she came up with another idea.

'Why don't you collect them back from me in Trittenheim yourself, on Saturday?'

I must have looked totally blank again.

'I'm inviting you to my wedding, stupid', she said. 'I've enjoyed meeting you, you've been nice to me and it would give me a chance to repay you for your company and the dinner and to return the Bottlang pages. Think about it anyway. You'll find us easily enough if you come. Trittenheim's a tiny little place and there's only one church. Wedding's at ten. See you then, I hope.'

She pulled on the helmet and the blonde pigtails vanished, but she gave me one more bewitching smile in response to my wishing her a good flight.

I watched from the warmth of the restaurant as she walked around the old Bücker, testing the taughtness of the rigging wires, checking the movement of the controls. I saw her swing herself into the cockpit, awkward in boots and flying suit, but still elegant with it. The engine coughed twice, then clattered into life. In a few moments my aeroplane was alone again on the hoar-frosted tarmac, the Bücker no more than a fading coloured light moving slowly among the myriads of stars.

I wasn't particularly worried about my Bottlang pages, and was sure Renata would post them back to me anyway, but the idea of seeing her again, even if she would be in the process of marrying some lucky German sod at the time, appealed to me. On the Friday, the forecast for the Ardennes and Luxembourg area was lousy; low cloud and poor visibility with occasional showers of rain or sleet. I decided to forget the gorgeous Renata and her wedding. Then I remembered it was only a couple of hours down the motorways through Brussels to Luxembourg and Trier. So I chucked my overnight bag in the car boot, and drove off, mentally kicking myself for being an idiot.

I passed through Trier just before eight that evening, relieved that I hadn't attempted to fly through the filthy weather. I followed the Moselweinstrasse along the banks of the river, through Mehring, past hillsides covered in dank fog-shrouded vines and into tiny Trittenheim where I checked in at the cosy little Gasthof. I soon forgot the weather outside as I sampled some of the local produce to wash down my supper.

Next morning it was still cold, but at least it was almost dry. With a raincoat over my good suit I walked along to the church. There was no sign of any wedding guests, no sign of any activity at all, in fact. I knew I hadn't got the time wrong. I could distinctly remember Renata saying ten o'clock. And she wouldn't have been in all that rush if the ceremony had been a week and a half away instead of just four days.

The pastor's house was next door to the church. He answered the bell himself, an elderly benevolent-looking man, traditionally dressed in grey with his ecclesiastical collar as a badge of identity. He assured me there had been no wedding planned for that day, nor for the next weekend, for that was the weekend before Christmas. What were the names of the couple?

Again I felt like an idiot. All I knew was the first name of the bride, a fairly common name in Germany too, so I volunteered a brief description of where and how we had met.

'Come in a moment, Sir', the elderly man said unexpectedly. 'Come in here and take a seat.' We settled ourselves on either side of a wood-burning stove in his book-lined sitting room. 'You say you met this Renata at Arnsberg airfield, and she was piloting a Bücker Jungmann?' There was a note of interrogation in his voice. I nodded.

'And when did this happen?'

'Tuesday. Last Tuesday evening. She took off for Trier at, let me see, it must've been around eight o'clock.'

For a few moments the only sound in the room was the tiny crackle of logs burning in their cast-iron crematory. Then the pastor cleared his throat with a slightly louder crackle and spoke softly.

'There cannot be many young girls with the name of Renata who fly a Bücker aircraft and know this little village.' I nodded again in agreement.

'Tell me, was she almost as tall as you are yourself, slender and with long, golden blonde hair?'

'She was. A very attractive girl.'

'Renata Müller. It has to be.' He paused for a long minute, then leaned forward towards me. 'But it cannot be. She would be almost fifty now, if she had lived. I buried her myself. Her grave is just across there.' He pointed out of the window to a little, steeply sloping cemetery between the church and the vineyards, then remained standing, his back towards the stove, looking down towards me where I was still sitting, stunned.

'Renata was a lovely girl in every way', he slowly said. 'She was a skier, a pilot, a graduate in history from Heidelberg, and was engaged to marry Dieter, son of one of the wealthier men in the village. She was flying herself down here from Hamburg just a few days before the wedding when she was killed in an accident just north of Trier. Our airfield in those days was down in the valley beside the Mosel river, quite close to the town. She crashed up near Föhren, very close in fact to where they've built the new airfield. So there is no way you can possibly have met Renata Müller. She's been dead for almost thirty years. She was buried on what should have been her wedding day.'

The sound of the burning wood remained undisturbed for several minutes. Finally the old pastor said, 'Are you all right?' I nodded once more, then rose.

'Perhaps I didn't meet her then, Father, but I just don't know. Could I see her grave, please?'

Together that grey morning we walked down the steep path between the gravestones. The old man stopped and inclined his head towards a squat marble slab with a flower vase in front of it.

'That is Renata's last resting place over there, Sir.' He turned and walked slowly back up the pathway. I read the inscription: '14th April, 1936 – 12th December, 1958 . . . as a result of a flying accident . . . beloved daughter of . . . Renata Ingrid Müller'.

There was, as is the custom in these parts, a framed photograph beside the stone. It was a faded photograph, but it was undoubtedly a photograph of the girl I had dined with five days previously. The same eyes and nose, the same high cheekbones, the same long blonde hair, flowing in the photograph, down over her shoulders.

'There isn't any explanation', I thought to myself. 'It isn't possible, yet it happened.' I was just about to leave the grave, the cemetery, the village and take my personal mystery with me when I noticed a scrap of paper wedged behind the photograph. I eased it out and unfolded it. It was the Bottlang landing chart for Trier Föhren aerodrome, with my own address written along the margin, in my own handwriting.

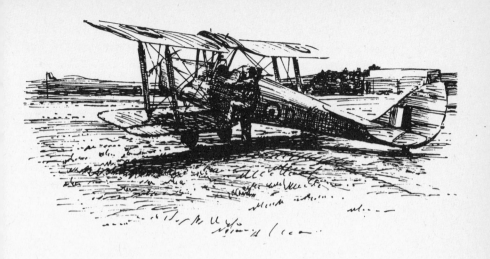

Chapter 6
PASSING STRANGERS

The London area forecast was that a warm front would move in slowly from the west that night, but the conditions for my early morning flight into Elstree were CAVOK. England positively sparkled in the winter sunshine as I flew in to attend a business meeting in the City. I glanced at the crowded traffic on the M1 motorway below me as I turned finals, and smiled. This was the way to travel. Just over one hour of flying certainly beat nearly four hours behind a steering wheel.

But the talking went on too long. There always seems to be someone on a committee who is so enamoured with the sound of his own voice that he has to ramble on for hours, contributing little, boring everyone, wasting time. By the time the chairman finally managed to conclude that meeting the warm front had swept in more rapidly than the Met Office had forecast and London was enveloped in mist, drizzle and low overcast. And so, as I ascertained by telephone, was my home airfield.

I was stuck in the Great Wen, at least until next morning, by when a ridge behind the front promised reasonable weather for the flight back. I telephoned the Spiders Web Hotel near Elstree to book a room, ready for an early morning take-off, and then faced the prospect of a long evening to kill in a cold, wet, miserable city.

To escape the damp I dodged into a couple of shops and looked around. My innocent browsing in a student-orientated book-shop was brought to an abrupt halt by a plump, dark girl with short-cropped hair, large-lensed spectacles and an unfashionable black dress peremptorily ordering me out at closing time. Had I been dressed in a sweater and faded jeans, carrying a parka, I wondered if she might have invited me to browse a little longer behind closed doors. But dressed as I was in a business suit and a burberry, carrying a flight case, I was quite definitely *persona non grata*.

The drizzle trickled coldly from my damp hair to find its way between the collar of my shirt and the skin of my neck. The legs of my trousers became soggy, slapping against my socks as I headed through the rain, looking for a taxi.

It was then that I saw the café. Despite the cold-blue fluorescence of its lighting it looked quite welcoming through its steamed-up windows. Once inside though, I felt my business suit and flight case even more out of place here than they had been in the bookshop.

I went to the self-service counter. As I collected a cup of pale coffee and a tired-looking sandwich, I felt every customer's eye in the place was on me; all eight eyes. I sat at a corner table near the window, watching the occasional rivulet of condensation trace its erratic track down the damp glass. The espresso machine built itself up to a crescendo of noise, like a One-Eleven on take-off. I breathed, rather reluctantly, the stale atmosphere of damp clothing, brown sauce, dirty ash-trays and cheap perfume.

The source of the cheap perfume departed, complete with her black, simulated-leather mini-skirt, long nylon-sheathed legs and plaited, bleached-blonde hair. Two minutes later she was followed by the only couple in the café, a sad, middle-aged lady wearing an incongruously brightly coloured sari, and her man, with short pepper-and-salt hair above a tired-looking mocca-coloured face.

The only other remaining customer looked across the café towards me with a tentative smile. He was elderly, wearing a heavily stained raincoat hanging open and trailing on the café floor. Under his dark-blue blazer with its frayed cuffs there was a beige woollen sweater with a cigarette burn on it. He badly needed a shave.

I ignored the smile and took a sip of coffee to help a mouthful of the dry sandwich on its way.

'Lousy night out, Sir.'

At least that was what it sounded like, but the voice was indistinct. After a pause I glanced across towards the man. The whites of his eyes were yellowish and veined with red, but the eyes themselves were of a penetrating light blue. There was, I thought, something vaguely familiar about them.

Our eyes met. He half-smiled again then slowly picked up his tea cup in one shaky hand, steadying it with the other.

I decided he was probably an alcoholic, looking for a soft touch for the price of his next bottle of cheap wine. I lowered the level of the coffee in my cup to below the half-way mark, then looked surreptitiously across the café again

There *was* an odd evasive familiarity about that face beneath the grey stubble, and in particular about those distinctive eyes.

He caught me looking again and opened his mouth to say something else. I turned abruptly away, gulped down the rest of the coffee and left the remainder of the sandwich. I had no wish to become involved with the old man, to be asked for a 'little something', even if it was nearly Christmas.

Gathering my burberry around me, flight case in hand I went back out into the rain without a backward glance.

I was in the taxi on the Finchley Road heading through the Hampstead puddles towards Elstree when I saw the stranger's face again, in my mind's eye. Much more clearly this time. The wrinkles of age were gone, the grey stubble clean-shaved. The eyes were no longer bloodshot. Their steady pale-blue gaze and the broad square forehead above them were in the setting of a young man's face. He was wearing a leather flying-helmet and goggles.

His name came to me in a flash. It was Leonard. He had been my first flying instructor, a Flight Lieutenant in the RAF some thirty-odd years ago; an idol of my younger years, the god who had imparted to my inexpert hands and feet the skills and techniques of his own craft and hard-won experience.

I told the taxi-driver to go straight back to the café near Charing Cross road. When I got back the place was empty. The stranger was gone, as was my half-eaten sandwich. The Italian proprietor said he knew nothing of the old man, had never seen him before.

I hope he hadn't recognised me. I hope he was just trying to bum a cup of tea from a passing stranger. I'd hate to think that he left believing I had deliberately ignored him. I, the ham-fisted pupil in the Tiger Moth to whom he patiently taught circuits and bumps, spins and recoveries, loops and rolls.

God knows, I owe him more than that.

Chapter 7
THEY ORDER THIS BETTER
IN FRANCE

There's something about the French way of life that makes it unique. There is a certain spirit, an ambience, an attitude of mind seldom encountered elsewhere. It all adds up to something that people of other nationalities either find wonderfully attractive or utterly unbearable. There are surprisingly few people who have an ambivalent attitude about France. Personally, I always enjoy visiting the country, and rarely turn down an opportunity of doing just that.

So, when one of the normally reliable hydraulic excavators built by a company I once worked for decided to confront its new owners near St Etienne with unusual ailments and this during the warranty period, no less – I wasn't too reluctant when my boss suggested I should go to France to diagnose and cure its sickness. In fact, he not so much suggested as insisted, and put some emphasis on speed of action, as each day's inactivity on the part of our product was apparently costing him untold thousands of francs. Surprisingly enough he even accepted my tentative proposal that I use my pilot's licence to save time by flying myself there, avoiding hours of delay changing planes at London and Orly. My cup of happiness was pretty well filled when I discovered the privately owned Comanche

250 which club members could use, was free for the next few days (and serviceable, too, what's more) and the duty forecaster gave me an unusually confident assurance that the anticyclone over Biscay would maintain beautiful VFR weather all over the relevant region for at least forty-eight hours.

I ought by this time to have been suspicious. It was all too good to be true. Little did I realise what new experiences of France lay just ahead of me. Still, we learn from experience, they say, and we live and learn too, so there's obviously a connection between life and experience, provided you live long enough to learn from the said experience. This little experience certainly was to add some new dimensions to my knowledge of the French way of life.

When the alarm shrilled off at 5.30 a.m. that June Tuesday morning I was awake much less reluctantly than is my normal wont a couple of hours later. I'd left time to change plans and use BEA and Air Inter had the Met Office been wrong, but a glance outside showed nothing more worrying than a vague morning mist that would obviously be shifted by the sun before I'd consumed my coffee and corn-flakes. The Biscay high was still doing its stuff.

At the airfield all was beautifully clear and silent. Early morning is a wonderful time of day; it's a pity you have to get up at such a godless hour in order to enjoy it. The route forecast I'd ordered was ready, and confirmed all was well. Customs were awake already, and cleared me outbound. The Comanche wings were slightly damp with morning dew, but after a pre-flight, and a wipe of her moist windscreen, she coughed into life, showed the right sorts of pressures, suctions and amperes and both VHF sets checked out strength five.

Just after seven o'clock Newhaven disappeared below the wing, and somewhere out there in the blue-grey morning sea haze were the cliffs of Cap Gris Nez. 'The further off from England the nearer is to France', as the lobster said to Alice. The old Comanche was running like a train. I suddenly realised that for the first time in my life I was actually savouring the joys of flying myself on business, at the company's expense. Hours into the log book without pounds out of the bank book; lovely! I was beginning to feel almost grateful to that chunk of recalcitrant hydraulic machinery waiting for me in St Etienne, when the French coast was there, and the Channel mistiness disappeared to leave what looked like all of France spread out before me. Wissant passed below the port wing, and my thoughts were off again back to the days of 1940 when Mölders and Galland took off from the grass airfield there and led their Bf 109's across to meet the Spits and Hurricanes of Fighter Command. Then I passed above the Somme near Amiens, with thoughts of an earlier war, seeing in my mind's eye the Camels and Spads and Fokkers and Farmans wheeling around the Comanche.

Then came Beauvais, with the memory of the ill-fated R 101 and from there I headed further south to keep clear of the Paris area, where I was sure I'd be too busy on the radio to day-dream pleasantly of Lindberg on his way into Le Bourget.

France really is a country full of flying memories, even for those who've never themselves flown there.

All good things, good flights included, come to an end, and this one ended with a professionally smooth approach and landing at an altitude of 1,350 feet on St Etienne's single north/south runway. The mountains further south shimmered invitingly in the warmth of the morning sun, and the odd cumulus above them were the only clouds I'd noticed all the way. Magnificent, I thought. What a way to do business!

Why the Douane required six hours' notice for the perfunctory customs formalities, I'll never know, but at least that meant I had arrived, ready for action on the right side of the frontier, as it were, by ten o'clock. And in these days, during the summer months at least, ten o'clock was the same time in France as in Britain. (Isn't it nice how being in the Common Market now, we're an hour out of step almost all the year through?)

Our customers were waiting for me, and with the Gallic unexpectedness typical of the French, greeted me, not with recriminations about bad British engineering, but with a demonstration of profuse gratitude at my expeditious attention to their humble problems. Also included in their welcome was an invitation to partake of a *pastis*, obviously essential before getting down to any serious business on a warm June day like this. I've often wondered what the boss would have thought, had he seen me at the start of my top-priority service engineering mission to France, perched on a stool at the airport bar, a Pernod in front of me, and a jovial French gentleman on either side, representatives of this irate and disillusioned customer of his. As I've said, the French and the British have a very different approach to things.

Eventually, of course, I renewed my acquaintance with the

machine that had left our factory but a few short weeks before. The customers were right. (Aren't they always?) It was showing every sign of being very sick and no sign of earning its expensive keep. Lunch followed this initial exploratory inspection. My boss had said, 'Stand them a good lunch whatever you do. It'll be worth the expense to get them into a better mood. . . .' 'So we ended up in a tiny café just down the road from where the machine wasn't working, ate crusty French bread off a red-checked table cloth, washed down the stew of the day with quantities of vin ordinaire and the customers paid the bill. I won't say they insisted; they just roared with Gallic laughter when I suggested it might be up to me to do the honours. No way. Not in France.

Despite the heat, the food and the wine my grey matter was still ticking over quietly when we got back to the real reason for my visit to France. I soon realised that Murphy's rule applied here once more. Two hose connections could be assembled the wrong way round, so naturally, after 'bleeding' the system to rid it of air one day, the mechanic had reconnected them arsy-versy. The net result was pressure in return lines, reverse flow through filters and sundry other circulatory diseases that resulted in some valves needing to be stripped, repaired and put together again. By seven that night the job was done, ready for a trial run in the morning.

My 'irate' companions insisted on keeping me company through another unsophisticated but delicious meal in the unsophisticated but acceptable hotel they'd selected for me. Then bed seemed very desirable after what had been a pretty crowded day.

The trial run went well in the morning. The machine was back in operation and everyone seemed highly delighted, especially my boss when I rang him to say I'd be home that night. The only slightly caustic comment came from the customer's own servicing fitter who suggested ever so gently but quite emphatically that maybe if we printed a service handbook for our export equipment in some language other than English it might save us some expensive time and travel. Touché. (I made the point when I was back in the office but so far as I know it never had had any effect.)

I managed to persuade my hosts that French lunches and French wine didn't make ideal preludes to flying, whatever their intrinsic attractions. I satisfied myself with an enormous long 'song-weetch de jambon' and a cup of aromatic strong coffee while my flight plan back to UK was maturing, and while I awaited the return of the customs man from his own lunch.

The sun was still blazing down on the concrete as I walked out to the Comanche, my jacket over one shoulder, my tool-kit in one hand, flight documents under one elbow and a carton of four bottles of local wine (by courtesy of the customer) in the other hand. It didn't occur to me that my little overnight case was still in the car that had brought me to the airport. Nor did it occur to me to go to the trouble of phoning the Met office in Lyons to check the weather situation, for wasn't it exactly like yesterday, and hadn't yesterday's flight been through perfect anticyclonic VMC?

The Total tanker topped up the Comanche's tanks, and the first substantial sum of francs that I'd had to spend that trip changed hands. Checks, start-up, more checks, taxi, run-up and take-off followed each other smoothly. As the Comanche and I clambered up through the warm air to find a cooler level that might reduce the greenhouse effects in the cockpit, I was already working out that I'd be back in England in nice time for dinner. And there was some wine in the back of the aircraft to add a soupçon of French flavour to the forthcoming English meal.

Everything seemed to be going just as beautifully as on the flight south when suddenly I realised that there wasn't any range of snow-capped mountains across north-west France. So these gleaming objects stretching horizon to horizon in front of me must be clouds. And big clouds at that. The left-hand end of what was obviously a frontal system seemed a lot higher than the right, so I did a bit of quick replanning of the route. I decided to cut north-east of Paris, via Reims to avoid the worst of the weather that way.

I tried to call Paris Info, to advise them of my route change, but, as often seems to happen with them, got no reply. I was beginning to feel a little lonely in the Comanche cockpit. All of a sudden, I remembered Volmet, and switched over No. 2 set to the Paris Radio frequency. As usual, they seemed to have got an Algerian, perhaps, who had learned his English from a Czech, to record the weather data. Furthermore, he'd obviously made the recording while chewing a croissant and in the background I could quite distinctly hear *saucissons* frying. All very appetising, but almost unintelligible.

The Seine passed beneath me near Troyes while I was jotting down those bits of weather I could hear. It wasn't too encouraging. Everywhere behind me was fine, Lyons, Zürich, Geneva, Nice, all 'more than ten kilometres' or 'CAVOK' but the two Paris airports (de Gaulle was still a mess of muddy concrete called Roissy in these days) were reporting one kilometer with around six oktas at 300 feet in rain. Charming. Brussels wasn't much better and although London was, that was of purely academic interest meantime, as there seemed to be no VFR way of getting there.

The cloud line was getting uncomfortably close now. The sun had all but gone and the thunderclouds towered menacingly in front. They weren't any less high than the ones in the south-west; they'd just been a bit further away.

I decided to divert to Reims (where they build the Cessnas, but probably would allow a Piper to ride out a storm). Then I realised that the 'Ghrime' airfield Volmet was talking about must in fact be Reims. And there was one thing for sure; I wasn't getting in there, either, now. It was even worse than Paris. Looking ahead I wasn't inclined to disbelieve them either.

Back towards Troyes then, I thought. But after a turn of about 90° I thought the better of it and swung back on my northerly heading. From out of nowhere, another squall line was lashing rain down on the hills I'd just flown over, and it seemed even nearer than the one to the north. Why the hell hadn't I got an up-to-date Met report that morning? It's amazing the situations a little bit of over-confidence can get you into.

The black wall of cloud and rain ahead was uncomfortably close before I saw the gleam of water that marked the River Marne. Somewhere down there my map assured me, was the little grass airfield of Epernay. Then just as I was giving up, I saw the road and railway and the airfield alongside them. The altimeter said 900 feet and the rain was lashing against the cockpit as I scraped the ragged underside of the storm clouds with the tail fin, and decided to land on 29 as directed by the T rather than the windsock, which had a more south wind look about it. It wasn't till after the wheels were on the welcome grass of the runway that I remembered I hadn't given them a call on spec., trying the standard 123.5 frequency used all over France by aero clubs.

At least I was down in one piece, and the aircraft had (and indeed was still having) a damn good wash, by courtesy of the weather gods. I taxied up near the control, switched off and sat listening to the racket of rain drumming on aluminium and perspex. After ten minutes the quiver had gone out of my legs, but the rain was as heavy as ever. Despite this I decided it was time to report in, so I collected myself and tried to collect my belongings, but convinced myself finally, after a prolonged search of the aircraft interior, that I really must have left my case behind in St Etienne. Of all the idiots!

Finally I steeled myself to it, opened the aircraft door, and bolted across the grass to the control building. For all the difference it made, I might as well have sauntered. My shirt was stuck to my skin and my trousers flapped damply round my ankles, dripping gently on to the lino. French rain is every bit as wet as the British variety.

My impetuous arrival had perturbed no one. No questions about lack of radio, just acceptance as a traveller looking for a place out of the way of the weather. Just as it should be. A phone call closed my flight plan and another checked that a room was available at a hotel near the local village of Plivot. I was offered a lift further, into Epernay itself where there a couple of top-class hotels, but I decided a bedraggled, damp, pyjama-less pilot might feel less out of place in a local hostelry than in a five-star country house.

My hotel, it appeared from a faded photograph at reception, was beautifully set among fields of vines from the grapes of which champagne is produced by the magnumful. The scenery I had to take on trust, for the deluge on the sun-warmed ground had produced mist now, and an unusually early dusk for the time of year.

There was no heating in the hotel of course, and I'd nothing to change into, so I ate early in my damp clothes and returned to my room with an armagnac to ward off a summer cold. A few minutes later the patron tapped on the door and offered me a pair of his slacks and a sweater to wear while his wife dried off my clothes in front of an electric fire. And that's service I doubt if I'd have got in a luxury hotel, even in France.

Two glasses of wine and two armagnacs later, back in my own dry clothes I was beginning to feel human again, and enjoying what little of the local patois conversation at the bar I could make out, until bedtime.

I don't know for certain what it is, but there's something in my nature that objects to sleeping naked. Even alone. Especially alone. Because of this, and despite the excitement of the day and the effects of the armagnacs I slept only fitfully. Maybe it was the noise of my beard growing against the sheets, and the knowledge that I'd nothing to shave it off with in the morning. Maybe it was my subconscious missing my routine brushing of teeth, or more probably nagging about that omitted route forecast. But finally morning came, and some of the other effects of wine and armagnac made their presence known, with a certain degree of urgency. I dressed, splashed some water on my unshaven face and went off in search of the toilet.

There appeared to be none near the bedroom so I returned to the little room beside the bar, which I'd used the previous evening. There were two doors. One was locked. The other opened and I found myself stupidly standing there looking at a gentleman in a situation normally reserved for strict privacy. He sat there, trousers discreetly pulled to just above his knees, his left arm resting on his thighs, and his right hand supporting his bowed head. It was for all the world as though he was pondering, perplexed by a problem of unusual depth. Slowly he raised his head and looked at me, with a face almost devoid of expression, while I for some reason just stood there, half awake. Then he spoke.

Had he been German or American, British or Dutch I would not have been surprised to hear some pretty forceful remarks involving some pithy epithets. But he was a Frenchman, who gently said:

'Pardon, Monsieur, ce n'est pas par manque de courtoisie, mais il n'y a plus de place.' (I've no wish to be inhospitable, but there just isn't any room.) Said quietly, politely and without a trace of sarcasm.

It may not have been original, but it certainly has stuck in my mind as another example of how different our French neighbours are from ourselves.

After attending to the demands of nature I washed a warm croissant down with a wide-mouthed cup of strong, hot coffee, and then mine host insisted on giving me a lift down through Plivot to the airfield where the aero club Les Ailes Sparnaciennes completed their hospitality to the stranded traveller by phoning in a flight plan and contacting Reims Champagne airport for (did you guess?) an up-to-date route forecast.

I had to land again at Le Touquet to clear customs, for that was one service even the friendly Epernay people couldn't provide, but that morning's flight was uneventful. Something seemed to have gone out of the joy of flying, however, as I returned, chastened, unshaven and somewhat wiser, across the Channel under some fair weather cumulus, back to base, and to the office.

During the couple of years I remained with that firm, the boss somehow never found it necessary to send me on any other business expense flights. But I know he often told potential customers about the service engineer's epic flight to St Etienne and instantaneous correction of the ailing equipment there – without, of course, mentioning the return journey.

For my part, it is largely the return journey that remains in my memory. Never since have I, and never again shall I, set out cross-country without a forecast. Nor shall I ever give up hoping that some day, if someone disturbs me as I disturbed my Frenchman on the toilet, I'll be able to remember his words, and the way in which he said them. But I don't expect it would sound as good in English.

As Lawrence Sterne once remarked, 'They order, said I, this matter better in France.'

Chapter 8
DELAYED ARRIVAL

It was a filthy night of foggy November drizzle when I checked in at
Sacher's Hotel in Vienna, so it wasn't long before I went down from
my room to the bar for a Scotch. And it was there that I met him,
appropriately enough, amidst the ornate surroundings in Sacher's
that belong to a bygone age.

My mood was as filthy as the weather. Business that morning in
Munich had dragged on and on, the ILS on my Baron was being
temperamental, and when I got the TAFs for Schwechat at lunchtime I decided to leave India Romeo where she was at Riem airport
in the hands of the avionics experts and to fly in one of the
scheduled services to Vienna. Unfortunately Austrian's evening
DC9 flight was fully booked and I was already too late for the
afternoon Lufthansa 737, so I'd been forced to endure an
uncomfortable jouney in an overheated railway compartment, a
chilly change of trains at Salzburg, and an expensive taxi ride the
length of a miserable, damp Mariahilferstrasse, all the way from
Vienna's West Bahnhof. A visit to Vienna with its atmosphere of
music and magnificent architecture normally cheers me up, but that
night the haloes around the mist-shrouded street lamps and the all-

pervading cold simply served further to deepen my mood of frustration.

Still, the brocades, velours and chandeliers of Sacher's bar were snug enough, and despite the price of the Scotch, I soon began to thaw out, physically and mentally. There was another solitary customer at the next table and I noticed he was wearing an RAF tie. Having heard him order a drink in English I decided his German must be even worse than mine, and after exchanging the usual surreptitious half smile that can be ignored or accepted as a sign an Englishman is willing at least to broach a conversation, we got talking.

It soon transpired that we were both pilots. He was earning his living as captain of an Aztec from Tyne Rapide Air, a North of England operator I had to admit I hadn't then heard of, and despite checking since, still cannot trace. Which was fair enough since he'd never heard of the little hydraulic specialist firm I run, and which in turn enables me to run the Baron for business, and occasionally also for pleasure.

A couple of drinks later and we decided we could put up with each other's company for dinner, and the evening eventually found us reminiscing over the coffee and cognac, of flying days of yore.

As the cigarette smoke curled slowly towards the ornate ceiling my mind began to try to fit together the bits and pieces of this man's flying career, as I'd learned them over dinner. I slowly became perplexed, for they didn't seem to want to go together.

He looked a good ten years younger than my fifty plus, and yet he'd started RAF training in Avro Tutors. In fact, when I mentioned India Romeo, my Baron he'd immediately spoken of another 'IR', a Tutor G-ABIR on which he'd logged many hours while instructing with Air Service Training at Hamble, and that certainly dated his licence into the early 1930s. For my part, the only biplane I've ever soloed is a Tiger Moth, and my flying days date from the mid-1940s when Oxfords, Wimpeys and Lancs followed the Tigers in rather rapid succession.

Either my wartime tours must have aged me prematurely, I thought, or he's extremely well preserved for the man of well over sixty that he must be.

That started up another train of thought; what about his wartime experiences? In all our chat, he'd breathed never a word about that little episode of his life.

Curiosity and the cognac getting the better of my discretion, I began to probe in that direction, to find if perhaps he'd spent these years as a POW or even possibly desk-bound for some obscure reason. He evaded the questions a couple of times, but then finally sighed, and said 'Buy me a good cigar and another brandy and promise not to interrupt with questions, and I'll tell you how I spent the war . . . but I warn you now, you'll probably regret the price of the cigar, for I don't expect you'll ever believe a word of it.'

Ten minutes later, the barman had ceremoniously lit the Coronas for us, and I settled back to listen.

He took but little time to cover his early flying years and confirmed that he had started RAF flying training in 1932 at the age of 20, so he was a great deal older than I'd imagined possible from his appearance. His first squadron posting had been to Iraq, but before he had even completed familiarization with the Wapitis in use there he'd contracted malaria, was in hospital in Habbaniya for weeks, then posted back to Blighty and in due course invalided out of the Service.

At least the RAF had seen him through the Depression years, and after shaking off the post-malarial weakness, he soon found summer work as a pilot of 'joy ride' aircraft (three-seat Tutors among them) at various holiday resorts. He added an instructor's rating to his licence, spent some time with clubs in the North and Midlands, then worked for a few months at Hamble, accumulating hours until he achieved his ambition and convinced one of Britain's embryo airlines that he was capable of captaining one of their airliners around the UK.

'My first scheduled service was in a Monospar and the passengers outnumbered the crew by just two to one', he told me. 'Two passengers and me!'

The bar was emptying now, and as his tale unfolded we had the place almost to ourselves.

'De Havillands took over in my flying life then, for after a year or so plugging away around Heston, Speke, Hooton, and Croydon in the old Monos, I heard of an opening with Midland Aerial Navigation, who were using Dragons on several routes from London to the Midlands and ultimately planned to link Renfrew and possibly even Dyce, which had just been opened, into the network, using the Dragon Rapide they had on order.'

As I listened to yarns of misty mornings over the Pennines and approaches to Croydon in London fogs that had all but stopped the buses, I began to feel ashamed at chickening out of a simple Munich-Vienna flight just because one of my six radio aids had been misbehaving slightly, but then I realised I was missing a new phase in the story.

'. . . so they gave me the job of proving the Aberdeen route in the new Rapide. G-AEOF was a superb new plane, much quieter and less draughty than the Dragons, and yet had a fair edge of speed over them. The trip north went like a dream, and I landed at Dyce a good fifteen minutes ahead of ETA. Next morning there was quite a send off – new plane, new service and all that. After a phone call to head office I got the okay to bring along, in addition to our two fare-paying passengers, a local newspaper reporter and his fiancee as well as the son of one of the local councillors. On condition, that was, that they'd be responsible for paying their own rail fares home. The boss had had dealings with Aberdonians before!

'Take off went well, but there was a lot of low stratus about that morning, so to avoid all the mountains south of Aberdeen I decided to route out over the North Sea at 1,000 feet, for a bit, before turning south to pick up the Northumberland or Yorkshire coast later. As we flew south, the gap between the waves and cloud base got less and less, until I decided it would be better to climb through it and hope the stratus would break up over England as the day got warmer. So we did just that, and enjoyed one of those idyllic trips in bright sunshine and clear, calm air at 3,000 feet with an endless sea of clouds below and a clear blue sky above.

'The passengers were fascinated – none of them had flown on top before – in the fact, the three "hitch-hikers" had never flown at all before. I was pretty fascinated too, with the smell of new leather and dope and oily metal that only a brand new plane has, and the hypnotic smooth rumble of the Gipsy engines and the steady flicker of the prop discs cutting through the sunshine. They don't build planes like that any more – more's the pity.

'We seldom used radio those days, but made occasional WT transmissions of position and so on, but that morning I could get nothing but static crackle from the set as I tried to report to Turnhouse and then East Fortune. Well, I thought, it would be too much to expect every item on a new plane to be in A1 condition at once, wouldn't it?

'I was scanning the clouds below for signs of the expected breaks when I first saw an odd veil of almost vertical cloud ahead. It stretched from horizon to horizon, east to west, and must have been 20 or 25,000 feet high . . . forever high, so far as the Rapide's ceiling was concerned. It didn't look like squall cloud, or normal thundercloud; in fact, it didn't look like any cloud I'd seen before, but smooth and translucent, if you know what I mean.

'We droned on steadily towards it. Closer to, it looked quite innocuous, so I decided that valour was the better part of discretion, and that there was no reason why we shouldn't fly through it. There was a slight up-draught as 'OF flew into the cloud, I remember, then a couple of little judders, then back to smooth air again. A few moments later I took my eyes off the instruments for a second, to check what the odd shadow was that we seemed to have passed through, and just then there was another shadow; a dark flash, if you can understand what I mean. This was followed by another and another in rapid succession, until it seemed someone was switching on and off a light – almost like the flicker of an old cinema film where everybody moves fast and jerkily, you know?

'Well, this went on for a while as a sort of blurred half light, but none of the passengers seemed even to notice – I suppose they all just thought it was a normal part of flying through cloud – and eventually it seemed to slow down again to a more distinct flicker before it stopped, just as suddenly as it had begun.

'There was scarcely a ripple of turbulence when we flew out of the cloud into clear blue above and unbroken white below, and everything was just as it had been north of the peculiar cloud – everything, that is, except another peculiar cloud of a type I'd never seen before. It was at an immense height this time, maybe 30,000 feet or more, and seemed to me like a straight white chalk line drawn across the sky. Most unusual it looked.

'But I was more interested in the cloud below, and the expected breaks were beginning to appear, so I knew I'd be able to let down through a hole and map read my way to Croydon. The first few gaps showed only sea, confirming that I must have drifted east, for by DR I knew I must be well south of 55°N and probably somewhere off the Lincolnshire coast, so I altered course, about 30° I suppose, to the west. Through another gap I saw a couple of fishing boats, and a minute or two later the coastline appeared in a series of brief glimpses.

'From my North Denes joy riding days around Yarmouth, I'd no hesitation in identifying the coast as just south of Cromer, and, with glimpses of the waters of the Broads through other cloud breaks to confirm my position, I worked out the probable wind, and estimated a course for Croydon. With just on one hour to run, the fuel state was fine, and it looked like being a snag-free proving flight.

'The radio still seemed U/S, with nothing but noises of frying bacon coming in, but I knew where I was, and since we were, if anything, a little ahead of time, nobody would be worrying about position reports.

'I watched out for any aircraft that might be on test around Martlesham Heath, but all I saw was the outline of the coast around Harwich and Felixstowe through the cloud. The odd unidentifiable length of road or railway showed up, and then I picked out the shape of Canvey Island and some murkier looking cloud that indicated the eastern outskirts of London.

'We'll be down at Croydon in another fifteen minutes,' I told my passengers. "I'm going to descend through this patchy cloud now, so you'll get a chance to see a bit of London", and down we went to about 1,000 feet through a gap south of the Thames, near Shooters Hill.

'It was shortly after that I began to realise there was something far wrong. I knew that part of south London better than the back of my own hand, and yet it seemed not quite right. There was a lot of suburbia going up very rapidly in the thirties but this was ridiculous; there below were whole estates that I didn't remember seeing before. Then, suddenly, I knew I was going mad; there was a row of skyscrapers, straight from the New York skyline over to my right, not two miles away.

'You'll never realise the feeling of blind panic that came over me then. Something impossible, unreasonable, unbelievable had happened. How? Why? I couldn't begin to think.'

He stopped and there was silence in Sacher's bar for a few moments, as if the horror of that far off moment was overwhelming him again. I motioned to the barman, who was now the only person left in the bar besides ourselves; and he, almost noiselessly replaced the empty brandy glasses with full ones. Suddenly the story was resumed, the emotions of the moment having passed.

'The Rapide seemed to me to be flying herself towards Croydon.

I suppose my hands guided her, but to be honest, I don't think I really wanted to get there. None of the passengers had been to London before, and they seemed very little surprised by what they saw. I think the only buildings they might have recognised in London would be the Houses of Parliament or Tower Bridge, and I told them we were too far south to see those – or Buck House either.

'When we got to Croydon I almost choked. It was quite unmistakably Croydon, with the hangars and the Brighton Road and the Airport Hotel but no damn airfield! Built up . . . all over it! Not a plane to be seen. . . . I tell you I was near to tears . . . panic, frustration, worry. I don't know what, but I could feel my palms clammy with sweat.

'Can you possibly conceive how I felt?' he asked. 'I'd been landing and taking off there twenty-four hours earlier, and now the damn place was all built up and destroyed. Can you even begin to imagine how I felt?'

There was another moment of stillness in the bar; we both inhaled another sip of brandy and then he continued.

'There wasn't any point in flying round the place in circles, and possibly adding suspicious or alarmed passengers to my problems, so I looked one more time at the erstwhile airfield just to be sure my eyes weren't deceiving me, and decided to set course for my alterate at Heston. As London unfolded a thousand feet below me, I became more and more thunderstruck. Architecture I'd never dreamed of, roads that didn't exist, clear areas where I remembered buildings and vice versa. I panicked again when the thought occurred to me – what will I find at Heston? The excited passengers suddenly recognised the Thames and a far-off view of Big Ben. I recognised Hammersmith Bridge and Kew Gardens and then, as I looked along the Bath Road towards Heston, I saw a mirage . . . a dream or a nightmare vision of ultra-modern buildings and vast roadways in a futuristic pattern with the silver shapes of peculiar aircraft dotted all over them. Not HP42s nor de Havillands nor Fokkers nor anything recognisable, but definitely aeroplanes of some kind.

'I steered the Rapide towards this incredible complex, trimmed her for landing lined up parallel to one of these immense roadways, and set her down on the grass beside it. At least we were safely on the ground again, I thought, but where on earth should I taxi to from here?

'Suddenly the sound of the idling Gipsy engines was drowned by an ear-shattering noise that caused the newsman's fiancee to faint . . . to tell the truth I damn near fainted myself as the first jet aircraft any of us had ever seen, a Pan Am 707 accelerated past us at full thrust on take-off.

'It felt like the end of the world, and in many ways, it was for me. Up till that day I'd captained my own life as well as my own aircraft, but from then on . . . well, there's not much left to tell. Several cars pulled up and surrounded the aircraft. Uniformed officials began to bawl me out as though I'd been caught with my hand in the till or something, and the six of us were driven off post haste in an ambulance of all things, with police and male nurses as escorts.

'I never saw that beautiful, brand new, Dragon Rapide again. In fact it was a long time before I ever saw much else at all again, except the inside of a psychiatric hospital.

'If I told this story once then, I told it a hundred and one times, to a hundred and one different people, police, immigration officials, doctors, psychiatrists and so on, but there wasn't one of them who believed me any more than I expect you do now. The simple facts are that we took off from Dyce in 1937 and we landed at Heathrow in 1959, and that, Sir, is where I spent the war years, not in any Stalag Luft anything, though I think I'd have much preferred that.

'My prison camp was the hospital, where they spent nearly three years trying to probe what had happened, and to find out where we six and our aircraft had come from. I gather two of the passengers are unhinged and still in hospitals somewhere and one of the others died when he realised the enormity of the whole situation and found it more than he could take. I was released eventually, as was the newsman's fiancee, whose memory had gone a total blank, but who's married now and the last I heard of her, in New Zealand, I think. She never even wanted to go back to Aberdeen.

'For my part I've tried to go back to anything and anywhere that will help explain what happened, but it's obvious that the authorities don't like unsolved mysteries, and have covered up all the evidence. Poor old 'OF the Rapide, it seems, was towed off to a hangar on the south of the airport, examined to see if it were a replica, or genuine, then secretly and uncermoniously scrapped. No one officially will admit to its existence now. There is no record of the landing, unless some reggie spotter has it as an entry none of his pals believe in his little log book. The Aberdeen Press & Journal and several other papers, local and national record the take-off at Dyce, and the mysterious loss, presumably in the North Sea, of an experienced pilot with five passengers in an ill-fated new aircraft, pioneering a new air route across the British Isles, or words to that effect. They searched for wreckage for weeks, but, eventually, of course, gave up.

'I searched for family for months, but had to give up too. My parents' home in Newcastle had been flattened in an air-raid and – not surprisingly twenty years after – nobody seemed to know or care if they had survived or not. Even if the bombs didn't get them, anno domini would have by now, and since I was an only child who'd been too busy flying to find myself a wife there wasn't anyone around who might be even remotely interested in my return from a watery grave in the North Sea.

'I'd no trade except piloting, and flying had altered almost beyond recognition, so I started again, with a new SPL and astonished my instructors with my aptitude for airmanship and stupidity about air law and radio. Eventually I got through the PPL, instructor's and instrument rating stages and up to where you can see me now.'

The weird tale had an odd ring of truth to it, the way he told it, but I saw one glaring inconsistency.

'How on earth did you manage to pay for your flying training', I asked him, 'when you can't have been exactly affluent on your release from the . . . ah . . . hospital?'

'The authorities did give me a sort of gratuity to see me started', he answered. 'I suppose someone reckoned it was better than having me resort to burglary or something, but as it turned out, they needn't have bothered too much. In Newcastle I went back to the savings bank I'd used and asked, tongue in cheek, for details of my bank balance, and do you know, I'd been saving for a car back in 1937, and had left £170 odd in savings. The company had credited my last month's salary to it, making nearly £200 in all, and that had been earning interest for a quarter of a century. There was just over £680 waiting for me, and with Tripacers and Condors available at less than £5 an hour, it was enough. I did a bit of evening work too, of course, to help pay the rent', he added.

It all added up now, and pieced together. It was completely impossible, of course, but seemed too true to be fiction, especially told in that way by that man, that night in those surroundings.

'I told you I didn't expect you to believe me', he suddenly broke into my thoughts, 'but thanks anyway for the cigar and the drinks. I'm off to bed, for even a young man of 65 needs his beauty sleep. Maybe I'll sleep sounder tonight for having got that lot off my chest for the first time in years. Goodnight.'

As he smiled, leaving the bar, I realised it was the first time I'd seen the tension leave his face, and felt almost annoyed when I noticed it made him look even younger.

I decided, late though it was, to indulge in one last drink while I mused over the extraordinary conversation of the evening. I was alone now, with the period decor and the young barman.

'*Verstehen Sie Englisch?*' I asked him.

'*Selbstverständlich*', he replied. 'It is an essential part of a barman's job in an international hotel like this, to speak English.'

'Did you by any chance hear that fellow's story?' I asked, knowing, of course, that he couldn't, in the otherwise empty bar, have avoided overhearing at least the latter part of it.

'Yes, Sir, indeed I did.'

'It was a strange tale,' I said. 'What's your opinion about it all?'

'Well, Sir', came the unexpected answer, 'I'm not really the person to ask for an impartial opinion, for you see, Sir, it was really me he came to visit tonight. He always does any time he's in Vienna – can't afford to stay at Sacher's, Sir, but always pops in for a drink, and to check up I'm all right. You see, Sir, if you remember, he told you the girl passenger had gone to New Zealand, one of the other passengers had died and two others were still in hospital. Himself included that makes five, Sir, and there were six on board, d'you remember?'

I suddenly was aware of a Buchan accent through his slightly Germanic pronunciation and even before he told me, I knew that this young barman in Vienna was the councillor's young son born in Aberdeen all these years ago.

It was still a miserable damp morning when, after a night disturbed by dreams of de Havillands disappearing into cloud formations, I emerged from my room for breakfast.

The story troubled me all day, breaking my concentration during business, and, I'm sure, costing me the contract I'd come to Vienna to clinch. I didn't lose the contract without a fight, however, and the discussions took so long I had to book for another night in Sacher's.

I went back to the bar after dinner, and found a different, older, barman on duty. I very much wanted to ask the one I'd met the previous night for the pilot's name, so enquired where I could find him. The elderly barman looked puzzled and said he didn't quite understand, for he'd been on duty there each night that week. Finally I discussed the matter with the assistant manager who assured me there was no young barman ever on duty in that room, as they believed an experienced and mature man was what their clients always preferred.

I was mystified. Surely I hadn't dreamt both the pilot and the barman?

I was booked on OS 411 back to Munich at 8.25 next morning, so I had an early night, but again not a particularly sound sleep, as I tossed and turned and tried to decide whether I was heading for a psychiatric ward somewhere myself.

The airport coach splashed its way along the dreary kilometres of petrol refineries and flat fields that lie between Vienna and Schwechat airport. Half awake I checked in, found gate 11 and got on board the DC9. Dawn had broken, I suppose, but under this perpetual overcast and drizzle it didn't make all that much difference to my half-open eyes.

We taxied out towards runway 12, and suddenly my eyes opened fully. Parked on the tarmac just alongside one of the maintenance hangars was an Aztec. I could read G-AV . . . but the last letters were obscured by someone loading luggage on board. What wasn't obscured were the words above the cabin windows 'Tyne Rapide Air', and as the DC9 attracted his attention the figure turned round and peered at it through the rain from under his peaked cap. It was him again, I swear it, and I'm not prone to dream things in airliners at half past eight in the morning.

Chapter 9
GALTIERI GESCHWADER

The long office was cool. From its marble floor to the pastel painted ceiling it had the feeling that, summer or winter, it would always have this slightly chilly temperature.

The young man moved uncomfortably in the tall chair in front of the desk. He nervously flicked his hair back off his forehead and concentrated on what the General was telling him. He shivered slightly, partly from the autumn chill, partly from anxiety.

The General rose to his feet and moved around the desk. To give emphasis to his words, he sat on the corner of the carved oak desk, placed his hands on the field-grey trousers of his uniform and leaned forward until his face was close to the younger man's.

'You understand what I've been saying?' His voice was soft, fatherly. It matched his silver-grey hair and the benevolent features of his tired-looking face. But it contrasted with the strength and fire in his penetrating blue-grey eyes.

The young man nodded. He tried to focus his gaze away from those eyes, to look at the gold oak leaves on the lapels of the olive-green uniform jacket, the red epaulettes carrying the insignia of General's rank, the gently clasped blue-veined hands resting on the grey-trousered knee. But some compulsion forced him to look again directly at the General, to subject himself once more to the force emanating from those eyes.

The gentle voice continued, persuasively.

'For years now we have looked after your people, helped you build here what you could no longer do in your own Fatherland. We have benefited from your efforts; don't think I'm not aware of that, and appreciative of it, too.' A pleasant smile flickered across the tired face, its friendliness marred only by the fierceness of the concentration in his steady gaze.

'The President is most kind.'

'No, not at all, Signor von Rothstein. Credit where credit is due. Much of Argentina's economic strength is due to the efforts of our many German friends.' President Galtieri allowed himself another gentle smile towards his visitor. 'As a spin-off, I realise, from your world-famous ability to develop industry for your own personal profit. I mean no insult', he added quickly, raising one hand as if to still any incipient protest, before continuing, 'I am merely being realistic. And we wish to go on benefiting mutually from each other's virtues of industry and, er, shall we say, assistance, into the future, too. You agree?'

'But of course, Mr President.' Walther von Rothstein was uncomfortable in the hard chair, in the cool office under the penetrating stare of the military leader of the Republic in which he had been born thirty-two years ago. That had been shortly after his parents had arrived there after a difficult and devious jouney that had started in Bavaria in 1945.

'Good! Then let me come to the nub of our discussion.' He slid back to sit squarely on the desk, steepled his hands, fingertips against his chin. The lines on his face changed imperceptably. His expression ceased to be paternal, and at last matched the aggressive eyes. The President had stepped again into the General's shoes.

'We have accepted you into our midst, your parents without asking questions, your own generation without asking for any more than we ask of our own young people. We don't ask you to pay unusual taxes, we have never discriminated against you. The German community in our country is an honoured portion of our population, despite some rumours and allegations of stigma in the past, despite some security problems you sometimes involuntarily present us with.

'But now, Signor von Rothstein, we are asking you for something. Something we cannot ask of our own people. And, for the good of continuing happy relations with our German friends in Argentina, I do hope you are going to be able to do for us what we ask.'

'If it is at all possible, Mr President, I assure you we shall.'

'In my career, Signor von Rothstein, I have never accepted anything to be other than possible. Sometimes things are more difficult, but always possible, provided enough time, or money, or effort or ingenuity is spent on them.'

The younger man automatically assumed that it must be a supply of the second of these factors that the President was leading up to. For a few years after World War II the German community in Argentina had been relatively impecunious, but since then, funds of strong Deutschmarks from Germany had augmented self-generated currencies in South America, to produce a very well-heeled ethnic group. He was fairly confident that through his own associates and some of the old guard still alive, he would be able to meet any financial demands the President was likely to make.

He relaxed slightly and with a deferential inclination of the head indicated he was ready to digest more of what President Galtieri had to impart.

'Our country is now having some difficulties with an old enemy of yours. Our economy is under strain. But it is something other than economic help I want from our German friends at this juncture, something altogether more in keeping with the military character and traditions your parents brought here with them back in the late forties.

The cool marble floor seemed to be sapping the last vestiges of warmth from the room. Walther von Rothstein took a deep breath of the chill air. So it wasn't money the old fox was after. What then?

'As I remember it, your late father was something of a national hero in the Luftwaffe, was he not?'

'I'm proud to say he was.'

'He led a Junkers Geschwader on many bombing expeditions over Britain before being transferred East?'

'Correct, Mr President . . . and he flew many missions over Russia before the Feldmarschall decided to use his tactical experience in directing operations against the Americans in France.'

'A father worthy of your pride, young man. And a tradition I am sure many Germans even today would be proud to see continued.'

The young man felt his leg begin to tremble. Was it this damn cold room, or the rise in tension as he began to get the drift of Galtieri's theme? He braced his foot against the floor, and tried to stop the nervous tremors.

'We've matched the English step for step, as you know. A century and a half after they seized our islands, we reclaimed them. They sank our General Belgrano, we knocked out their Sheffield. They shot down our Skyhawks, we downed their Harriers. Blow for blow to defend our Malvinas, and we plan to continue for as long as it takes until the myopic world sees the justness of our cause. We are a nation awakened, a nation united!' His whole being became as animated as his piercing eyes. He raised a tightly clenched right fist in front of von Rothstein's face.

'But there is one area in which we are powerless to match the English', he continued, in a tone better suited to announcing a triumph, 'And it is to counter this threat that I am calling upon you.'

'*Gott in Himmel*! Not nuclear weapons?' von Rothstein gasped without thinking.

'No, I don't think even the Iron Lady's mind has rusted to the point where she would consider it worth plunging the world into atomic warfare to save her political reputation. No, young man, but there is another more probable eventuality. Sooner or later the English are going to attack our beloved mainland of Argentina. Sooner or later we are going to suffer bombs or saboteurs at Rio Gallegros or another of our mainland airfields, at Ushuaia or another naval base or even maybe on Buenos Aires itself. We have evidence that there are already several RAF Canberra bombers based in Chile, carrying Chilean markings. And we have no means of retaliation against Portsmouth or London or anywhere else. We need allies for that. Secret allies. German allies.'

'But Mr President, there's no way anyone here could do anything to . . .'

'Senor . . . or rather Herr Major Walther von Rothstein, for I am aware of your courtesy title in the 4th Reich Movement . . . you have your contacts back in Germany. Powerful contacts, influential contacts. Remember, I do not believe in impossibilities. And remember that in this country it is I who have the power, and the influence.'

He slid lightly off his desk and extended his right hand, fist now unclenched. The German was surprised to find the President's hand so warm when he shook it, signifiying the end of the audience. His own was like ice.

'There is an office with direct international telephone access at your disposal in the Defence Ministry. Amadeo Frùgoli is expecting you. And I am expecting a positive report from you five days from now.'

The warm hand released the cold one. President Leopoldo Fortunato Galtieri walked round behind his desk again, resumed his seat and began to read a telex. Walther von Rothstein, still wondering if it was all a bad dream, made his way to the heavy, panelled door.

Five days later it was a much more confident German who rang the President's secretary from his temporary office in the Ministry of Defence in Buenos Aires. President Galtieri accepted his report impassively, then showed awakening interest and finally enthusiasm.

'Young man, after a week of nothing but incompetence and set-backs in the Malvinas, it is good to have a bit of encouraging news at last. I like your plan. I like the level of contact you have managed to arrange, and more than either, I like your embellishment of my plan. Your pre-emptive strike is undoubtedly, in this context, much to be preferred to a mere retaliatory blow, provided it does not jeopardise a follow-up if needed.'

'I'm sure our colleagues have covered that aspect of it, Sir. There is more than one way into London's air defences these days. We'll use one for the first strike, and for the follow-up, if any, we'll make use of a totally different technique.'

'Then time is of the essence. Get over there yourself, if necessary. Co-ordinate your colleagues and get our first aircraft over England before they launch a Vulcan from Ascension Island against Comodoro Rivadavia, Puerto Belgrano or us here in BA.'

★　　★　　★

Shortly after ten in the warm June eveing, Lieut. Horst Brandenberger was studying the notes he had scribbled down after his recent surprise telephone conversation with his Officer Commanding in Germany. It didn't make sense. He moved from the table to the easy chair in his room in the Officers' Mess of RAF Cottesmore where he was just completing his operational con-versation training on the Panavia Tornado aircraft. He read the notes again. Has the OC gone crazy? Here I am in England, training alongside British pilots and yet now under secret orders to prepare for a raid on central London.

The call he had been instructed to make back to the OC would confirm if it wasn't a hoax. But then? Lieut. Brandenberger was a well-disciplined methodical German pilot. He digested the unpalatable information, made the phone call as instructed, received amplified orders, and began to prepare himself for the task ahead. The necessary equipment would be arriving from Germany on Thursday. He had forty-eight hours to ready himself for the operation and also to pass his final handling test under the eagle eyes of his Royal Air Force wing commander.

★   ★   ★

Several owners of aviation museums around Europe had been surprised, perplexed or astonished, depending upon their moods at the time, to receive telephone calls enquiring if they happened to have an airworthy Canberra as an exhibit, and if so, whether they would be willing to sell, price being of little object. The caller's voice had a vaguely American accent, with foreign overtones, like the voice of a second-generation New York upper-class immigrant from Europe. In each case the answer he got was in the negative. Canberra bombers are thirsty brutes to fly unless you have the resources of an air force budget behind you to pay the fuel bills.

Claude Delavier, one of the collectors contacted, with an idea of at least sharing in what might be a fat profit, asked for a number to call back after he had checked around. He was abruptly told he would be called back exactly twenty-four hours later.

He spent the day phoning colleagues, collectors and some contacts he had in the international arms business. It wasn't long before he found his American-voiced caller had called many more men in the business than himself.

'What's all the sudden interest in a Canberra?' was the question several people asked him, and he asked himself the same question, more than once.

Then it happened. He found it. Officially non-flyable, it was on its way to a metal dealer's yard in the Middle East, its engines time-expired, its airframe a little tired. But its last owners had flown the Canberra only a few weeks earlier, so presumably it could be made to fly again, albeit illegally.

The scrap merchant named a price, exactly five times more than he had paid for the old aircraft. Claude added fifty per cent for himself and waited for the phone call.

When it came there was no haggling. Just a pointed threat. The caller agreed the price without demur, on the one proviso that the machine would fly. He also insisted on collecting it himself.

'But how do I get paid?' wailed Claude.

'In used 500 franc notes if you tell me where the machine is now, Monsieur Delavier, or in lead through the kneecaps if you try any nonsense. We know where to find you. Now tell us where to find the bloody bomber.'

To his surprise, Claude received an unregistered parcel several days later. He counted the grubby notes inside. They totalled precisely what he had asked for. He drank an extra-early, extra-strong *pastis* that morning. It was the most unusual business transaction he had ever been involved in.

★   ★   ★

At Cottesmore, Lieut. Brandenberger met his OC after his arrival from Erding Airfield in Germany. After public congratulations on the successful completion of his Tornado course, Horst was treated to a very private discussion of the operation to be carried out. The necessary supplies had been brought across to England in the OC's aircraft. The two men would transfer them to the Tornado that Friday night, and early on Sunday morning Horst was to take off.

Once all flying at Cottesmore had ceased for the weekend, all the aircraft were picketed in blast shelters or towed into lofty wartime hangars and locked away to await Monday morning. It was a Tornado in one of those hangars, close to which the OC's aircraft was parked, that Horst selected for his mission.

The two men loaded the bomb-bay of the Tornado, then covered the red, white and blue roundels of the RAF insignia on the wings, sides and tail of the aircraft with blue and white decals, and horizontal blue and white stripes of self-adhesive plastic on the fin and rudder. The Trinational Tornado Training Establishment at Cottesmore had, all unknowingly, acquired its first Argentinian Air Force aircraft.

'I'm glad we're using a British registered machine, and not one of ours', the OC explained. 'Our *Kameraden* were quite insistent that there should be as little connection as possible between this job and our Fatherland.'

Horst signified his agreement.

'You realise', the senior officer continued, 'that I, or rather we, are not involved in this in support of the Argentinians? *Mein Gott*, Horst, I wouldn't even cross the street to save one of their miserable skins. We're in it for the sake of our own fellow Germans, heroes of our past, and descendants of those brave men, condemned by circumstances to live outside Germany, and now threatened by this upstart junta. It's for Germany we have been asked to do it, you understand, not for the Gauchos.'

On Saturday morning the OC's aircraft departed for its base at Erding, with Lieut. Horst Brandenberger listed as one of the personnel on board. He went through the customs formalities, but slipped around the aircraft into a hangar office, leaving his OC to depart, as planned, without him.

While the Tornado pilot spent an uncomfortable night keeping a watchful eye on the Argentinian-decorated aircraft, locked up for the weekend in a dark, secure hangar, two other Germans were spending an equally uncomfortable and rather more exciting night ferrying a theoretically unflyable Canberra across the Mediterranean and over Europe.

Fully fuelled, they had coaxed the old bomber off a hot, sandy desert airstrip at dusk, and since then had been masquerading as a civilian Lear Jet on its way from Cairo to Luton, so far as radar operators and air traffic controllers were concerned. After hand-over from the French controllers, they maintained radio silence instead of contacting the British, then descended rapidly to low level and headed north-east up the Strait of Dover into the North Sea. Skimming the water, below the cover of the radar scanners, they crossed the Belgian coast, continued low over the flat landscape until, between the ancient cities of Bruges and Ghent, the pilot spotted what he was looking for. Four sets of car headlights were switched on, faintly illuminating a huge concrete runway.

Engines throttled back to disturb as few locals as possible, he pulled the Canberra round on a wing-tip to line up with the runway, downed the flaps and undercarriage and landed safely by headlamps augmenting the aircraft's landing lights.

The driver of a blue Mercedes leaped out as the Canberra rolled to a stop. He drew his hand across his throat urgently, imploring the pilot to shut down the engines and silence their roar. They had arrived at the NATO emergency airfield of Ursel in Belgium. Minutes later the bomber had been towed by a farm tractor, off the runway, up a dispersal road, through a gate and into a clearing in the thick pine forest that surrounds this usually deserted aerodrome.

'Well done, lads!' A German voice greeted the two men as they stepped stiffly from the cockpit. 'She's well hidden here. We'll redecorate her tomorrow night in the appropriate colours, then fuel her up. The bombs are already inside Belgium in a truck laid up awaiting orders in the Ardennes. We can fly the mission any time after tomorrow night, given eight hours notice.'

The weary crew settled into the back seat of a big BMW for the long autobahn trip back to their homes in Bavaria.

Meantime the air-sea rescue services began a fruitless search for a missing Lear Jet, believed to have come down in the English Channel somewhere north of Cherbourg.

★   ★   ★

As the Canberra crew completed their job, Horst Brandenberger steeled his nerves to commence his. Like most RAF airfields, Cottesmore dies over most weekends. RAF policemen with dogs patrol from time to time, but little else disturbs the stillness. As the morning mist became visible in the early light of dawn on Sunday, Horst unlocked the hangar doors and cranked them slowly to the fully open position. Nothing else moved. No sounds or stirrings over by the living quarters indicated that anyone had observed the movement.

The vicious-looking nose of the Tornado now pointed straight towards the airfield beyond the hangar opening. The Argentinian markings looked odd in the silvery light of a June dawn. Horst climbed into the cockpit, clad in parachute, safety gear, anti-g suit and all the paraphernalia of a jet fighter pilot. He connected everything up.

Now all he had to do was wait. His orders were to start up and take off at 0800 or earlier if necessary, depending on whether anyone noticed him before then.

No one did. Two policemen with dogs passed diagonally across the airfield half a mile in front of the open hangar. Neither remarked on the doors being open, neither noticed the odd markings on the aircraft. Horst remained still and silent in the cockpit until the time came to commence the engine-starting cycle.

At 0755 the Sunday stillness and silence of the Lincolnshire countryside was shattered as the Tornado's Rolls-Royce turbines spooled up and blasted dust and decibels out of the hangar and across the deserted airfield.

Horst released the brakes, edged the big fighter-bomber past the hangar doors, then opened the throttles for a rapid dash round the perimeter track towards runway 23. As he reached the start of the runway he saw an RAF police Landrover heading across the grass towards him. He slammed the throttles forward, released the brakes and, as the Tornado accelerated away from the vehicle, selected afterburners 'on' and lifted into the air on a fiery tail and an ear-splitting cacophony of sound.

NATO's defence system is not at its most alert in the early morning hours of a Sunday. Signals were darting to and fro concerning the theft of a Tornado aircraft, North Sea coast radar units were being rudely awakened to red-alert status and fighters on stand-by in various European countries were suddenly crewed and started up.

But from Cottesmore to London is only ninety miles as the Tornado flies. And ninety miles took Horst less than seven minutes to cover as his afterburner thrust pushed the aircraft supersonic, its wings now swept back into a near-delta plan form as it blasted low across the sleepy English counties.

From north to south it shot across Hyde Park and the Thames followed by the double thunderclap of its sonic boom, and the screaming howl of its engines. No one in central London slept later than 0808 that Sunday morning.

Horst felt the anti-g suit squeeze his legs and abdomen as he pulled the Tornado round in a tight turn, low across Wandsworth and Wimbledon, Richmond and Brentford, cutting a swath of supersonic sound across the capital. Over Hammersmith he straightened up and accelerated again, to pass over the Serpentine, the City, Bethnal Green and Barking within seconds of each other, a jumbled kaleidoscope to him, a din like the clap of doom to those on the ground.

It was now ten minutes since take-off. Pursuit must be nearly under way. Obeying orders, Horst slowed down below sonic speed over east London, extended the wings to the slow speed configuration, displaying their Argentinian roundels to advantage, and then, bomb-doors open, flaps extended, he eased the big machine majestically and slowly back west up the Thames. Over Waterloo Bridge he began pressing the bomb-release buttons. The final one he triggered off as Downing Street and Westminster disappeared below his wing. The bomb-doors snapped closed, the flaps retracted, the vicious afterburner flame lit up and the Tornado, sweeping its wings back once more, streaked supersonically farther and farther west, rudely awakening half the citizens of south-west England as it went on its noisy way.

It also wrong-footed the Lightnings and Falcons and Hornets being scrambled all around Europe, all of whom assumed the stolen aircraft would be heading east.

Instead it landed, unannounced, at twelve minutes to nine on a still somnabulent Shannon Airport in Ireland. Its pilot leaped from the cockpit into the passenger seat of a Volkswagen Scirocco that was waiting for him close to the boundary of the airport, far from the terminal and industrial area.

'Did it go all roit, man?'

'Like clockwork. Just as it was planned.'

'Thanks be to God! The *Kameraden* will be pleased.'

'And relieved too, I would guess.'

In Limerick, Horst transferred to a Ford Granada; in Cork he was just in time to catch the Aer Lingus Boeing to Paris at 1325, on his way back towards Germany.

The leaflets that had cascaded over London that morning through the pandemonium, into the hands of frightened, half-asleep and perplexed people, had been printed in Buenos Aires. The English was not grammatically perfect. But their meaning was abundantly clear. It had only been paper this time, but if they were forced to do it a second time, the Argentinian Air Force would then drop something more substantial than pamphlets on London.

The Canberra to do it with lay hidden in the coniferous forest of West-Flanders, its potential crew at readiness in Bavaria, its bomb-load concealed in a remote corner of the Ardennes.

★   ★   ★

Leopoldo Fortunato Galtieri, ex-President of the Republic of Argentina groaned as the pain in his back, induced by the hard prison mattress, half-roused him from his dream. He winced and ground his teeth together.

'If only Frùgoli hadn't been so short-sighted, so set against it', he muttered to the peeling paint on the walls of his cell. 'If only I'd gone ahead with the plan to put pressure on the *Kameraden*, I'd still be President today. President of Argentina *and* the Malvinas.'

He rolled over and closed his eyes again, trying to pick up the thread of his dream, trying to escape the wretchedness of reality.

Chapter 10
ARNHEM AFTERMATH

A bead of perspiration trickled slowly over Bert's shoulder and across his back. It felt like a lover's finger against his warm skin. Sleepily he brushed it away with his hand and tossed into another position on his mattress below the mosquito netting.

'My God', he said. 'It's bloody hot; and dark; and humid.'

Beyond the filmy netting he could hear the high-pitched whine of the mosquitos, scenting his body, thirsty for his blood. And beyond that thin whine which rose and fell in pitch as the insects vainly sought an ingress to their target, came the all-pervading nocturnal sound of the jungle.

At first the harsh cries, the jabbers of incoherent animal voices, screams as of pain and strident bird calls had frightened Bert. But that had been over thirty years ago. Now they were no more than a background to his life, unnoticed, indeed unheard, except on nights like this when the pre-monsoon sticky heat, or maybe indigestion, was keeping him awake.

He rolled over again, seeking a comfortable position. Instead, he gave himself a jab of pain as his weight landed on the stump of what had once been his right arm. The nerves jangled all across his shoulder.

'Damn yourself for an idiot', he muttered. 'After all this time you ought to know not to thump your stupid stump like that.'

His mind went back more than three decades. Back to his nineteenth birthday, on 17th September 1944. Instead of a party that year he celebrated the event by taking part in operation Market Garden. It was still all as clear to him as yesterday.

The slap on the shoulder from Scotty as they lumbered out to the rows of aircraft after breakfast, loaded down with kit, equipment and parachutes.

'Many Happy Returns, Bert, y'auld bastard!'

Scotty had remembered.

'One happy landing'll do me this year.'

'Aye, y're dead right at that, too.'

But it hadn't been a happy landing for either of them. The pilot of their C-47 Dakota illuminated the jump light seconds too late, and instead of coming down over Arnhem, Scotty and Bert drifted helplessly on their chutes into wooded country, infested with the enemy. Scotty landed cleanly, dumped his chute, collected two comrades and all three were cut down by a German machine-gun only minutes later.

Bert heard the rattle of the gunfire from where he hung, suspended by the tangled rigging and canopy of the parachute from an upper branch of a Dutch pine tree. It was too far to drop, carrying the weight of his gun, ammo and the rest of his kit, so he jettisoned it all to the ground, then slammed the quick-release on his harness. It was jammed. He twisted it and pressed, pushed and punched it, all to no avail.

He hung there, helplessly, the drizzle gradually penetrating his camouflage clothing.

Two figures appeared close by below him. He was about to call out when he realised he was looking down on German helmets. They disappeared again into the forest. Bert grappled in his battle-dress pocket for the emergency knife all paratroops carried just for occasions like this, to cut the harness free. The pocket was empty. He didn't believe it. He groped for it again, but no knurled handle was to be felt, no well-known shape of blade or sheath.

'Great God almighty', he mouthed silently, 'What did I ever do to merit this.'

He was still hanging there, cold and wet, when another German appeared. This one tripped over Bert's rifle, looked around himself, suspiciously, then glanced upwards. Before Bert could react the German aimed his automatic rifle vertically up towards Bert and released a stream of lead at him. The bullets tore into his right arm. Mercifully he lost consciousness.

It must have been the pressure of Bert's parachute harness against an artery in his armpit that prevented his bleeding to death. It was mid-afternoon before his body with its pulverised arm was cut down from the tree, found to be still alive, and ambulanced off to a German field hospital near Doetinchem.

That was the end of Bert's war. It was the end also of his job as a joiner and his favourite sport, golf. It was the end of Bert and Sybil, too. Once he got home from POW camp he found she preferred boys who could jive, and who could appear in public without attracting odd, sidelong glances at a pinned-up sleeve.

The rehabilitation people found Bert one dull job, then another boring one and a third mindlessly monotonous occupation to eke out his disability pension. He gradually became less self-conscious about the permanent leather glove covering the ghastly pink of the plastic hand that protruded from his right sleeve, but helping in a florist's back-shop, or pumping petrol into Morris Minors seemed to be less than satisfying ways of spending the rest of his life.

★　　★　　★

Outside, the jungle noises of the night continued unabated. Inside it began to feel warmer and stickier than ever. Another rivulet of sweat ran across Bert's shoulder blade, tickling like an insect's feet as it went. It was almost four o'clock, and he cursed the heat and the sleeplessness, thinking of another strenuous, even hotter and equally humid day, ahead. It was September 17th again, but he had long ago stopped counting his birthdays.

He might have been better to put up with England after all, filling-station forecourts notwithstanding. At least it wouldn't have been as clammy as this. But he had made his decision many years ago, and had survived the monsoon seasons every year since. He'd survive this one, too.

'Keep your nose clean and you could end up running the plantation', his chance contact in the pub had said. It was a wintery day in Wakefield. The garage forecourt had been covered in slush and clearing it with only a left arm to work with was no fun. The idea of warmth and sunshine, the thought of willing native girls and memories of scenery from the film *South Pacific* had been irresistible. Bert grasped the opportunity to escape from post-war England.

There had been willing native girls, too. Several over the years. And tropical warmth and sunshine as well as monsoon rains. And the promised promotion had come. The one-armed outcast had become manager of the plantation, with a loyal staff to do all the work that a disabled man found difficult.

Following independence, his was one of the few posts still occupied by a European. It made things a bit lonelier, but Bert was a bit of a loner anyway, and having nothing to go back to Britain for, he felt he would have been even lonelier there.

He grabbed at his pillow and flicked it the other way up. Momentarily that side felt fractionally cooler, less sweat-soaked. Gradually he felt sleep floating back towards him.

Suddenly he was wide awake again. Far beyond the thin whine of the mosquitos and just becoming audible over the usual background noises from the jungle forests, was a new sound. He propped himself up on his elbow to allow both ears to function.

The noise was more distinct now. A soft, pulsating sound, fading, then strengthening again until Bert was quite sure it was an aircraft. It had a deep, throaty roar to it, quite unlike the banshee whistle of the military jets that occasionally flashed across the hilly plantation, or the attenuated jet noise of the civil aircraft that painted thin white chalky trails across the blue of the tropical skies.

It certainly wasn't the burble of the Islander that came twice weekly on its peregrination around the jungle landing strips, or the high-revving engine note of the little Cessnas that buzzed across the jungle sky in diverse directions taking pilots and passengers about their lawful and unlawful business. Nor was it the throbbing, drumming note that emanated from the helicopters that sometimes brought in supplies when the tracks were all washed out and the rivers flooding over their banks.

It was a sound he remembered. One he hadn't heard for a long, long time. Then the penny dropped. He was back in Europe again, back in World War II. That was the sound of a Heinkel in the blitz, of a Lancaster in flight over Yorkshire, Berlin bound, of an only-just-still-Flying Fortress, staggering back in tatters from Turin.

These were heavy piston engines droning through the night. Real aircraft engines. Just like those that had powered the Whitleys and Albemarles he had flown in during his parachute training, just like the powerful radials that dragged the Dakota that had flown Scotty and himself and a couple of dozen others to Arnhem on his nineteenth birthday.

The aircraft was almost directly overhead now. The powerful rumble of its engines began to die away as it headed on through the velvet darkness of the humid sky towards wherever it was bound.

The unusual sound brought back memories to Bert. He felt again the swaying tin-sided fuselage that sloped steeply upwards as the paratroops boarded on the airfield, but was perfectly horizontal when they left it in flight. He heard again the metallic click of the static-lines being fastened, saw again the half-eager, half-apprehensive grins on the blackened faces beneath the tin helmets. He could sense again the mingled smells of 100-octane fuel, aircraft paint, new sackcloth, gun-oil and the sweat of frightened men that always seemed to permeate the Dakotas of the 1st Airborne Division.

Then the sound stopped. It didn't fade away imperceptibly in the way it had risen to its crescendo of pistons and valves and exhaust stubs. It just suddenly stopped. Bert sat up in bed. Before he was fully upright a dull detonation boomed across the plantation. Some cups rattled on a shelf next door.

The echo of the explosion came from the hills on the other side of the valley about eight seconds later. There was a momentary total silence and then the natural sounds of the jungle slowly reasserted themselves.

'Ako!' called Bert to his 'boy', who was scarcely ten years his junior and had been with him ever since he had become plantation manager, but whose four-syllable native name Bert still couldn't get his tongue around.

'Yes Mister Bert, Sah.'

If he had been sleeping Ako could only have been in a very light sleep.

'Did you hear that noise?'

'Ah shore did, Mister Bert, an' Ah see de light, too.'

'You saw the lights of the aircraft?'

'No, Sah, but Ah can see de light now.'

Bert pulled on a dressing-gown, more as an anti-mosquito measure than in the interests of decorum, and joined Ako where he was standing on the verandah.

On the eastern horizon, where the Nikagwe hills ranged above the jungle-covered floor of the valley there was indeed a light. It was a reddish-yellow light, flickering in intensity, and through his binoculars Bert could distinguish far-away wisps of smoke as the flames of the fire illuminated them.

'Poor bastards', he said quietly. 'There's nothing anybody can do for them until daylight, and not much anyone's likely to be able to do even then. But we'll have to try.'

Ako moved quietly off, leaving Bert to watch the flames slowly die. He took a compass bearing of the scene of the accident, then dressed. Within a few minutes Ako returned, this time in the Landrover, complete with an inflatable boat in the back, machetes and climbing gear.

'You have the map, Sah?'

Bert had, and he already had the bearing pencilled in on it.

'If the crash is on the first of the Nikagwe ranges we should be able to reach it before midday', he said, as Ako drove the Landrover off in the direction of the river, 'But if it's up on the main ridge, it'll be a job for a helicopter.'

From the river's edge the hills stood out clear and sharp, only a few miles away, silhouetted against the early morning sky. They launched the boat, paddled it across the broad yellow stream and hauled it well up the mud-banks on the far side.

The tough bit began now. Ako led, through the grassy lands, into the bush, and along the animal-tracks between the jungle trees. They took turns at hacking undergrowth and creeping vines that blocked their way, and ultimately reached the foothills.

Almost at the top of the first range Ako spotted a darkened area of trees. Bert trained his glasses on it and confirmed that it looked like a burnt patch of forest. It was exactly on his compass bearing.

Before eleven o'clock the two men were standing exhausted in the heat of the still-climbing sun, beside a crumpled, burned-out wreck.

'They never had a chance', Bert said quietly, looking at the shattered remains of the cockpit and front fuselage section, twisted out of recognition by the impact and the intensity of the flames.

Ako nodded in agreement.

Beside the fragmented fuselage were the charred remains of a huge radial engine and a badly mangled wing. The other wing was nowhere to be seen. Buried, no doubt, somewhere amidst the trees and creepers, ferns and undergrowth somewhere further down the hill.

The only identifiable piece of wreckage that had escaped the fire was the tail-assembly, broken away from the fuselage close to the main door. It lay askew on the mossy green flank of the hill, maybe thirty paces from the cockpit that had become the crematorium for the crew.

The two men walked the thirty paces. Bert noted down the registration letters painted on the aircraft's tail, then stood, his head cocked to one side, trying to line up the shape of the fin, and see what it would have looked like on an even keel.

It couldn't be. Or could it? There were still some of them in service after all these years, and that swept-back leading-edge, blunt tip and huge straight-edged rudder could only have belonged to a Dakota. No wonder that engine note had reawakened old memories.

Ako clambered into the wrecked tail and looked around.

'Nuttin' here, Sah. Nuttin' at all.' He knelt on the floor and peered into the space between the aircraft flooring and its outer belly-skin. There was moss and gravel wedged in it, rammed into it during the final violent contact with earth. Ako dislodged a handful of moss. Some loose material trickled and rattled out after it, and then another object, larger and longer than a piece of gravel, clattered out amidst the rest. When the shower of debris stopped, Bert moved forward and picked up the long object.

He stood rigidly staring at it, unbelieving, as it lay inertly in his left hand. He closed his fingers slightly and ran his forefinger over the knurling on its hilt, his little finger touching the decaying leather of the sheath around the knife blade. He knew it *couldn't* be the one he had lost at Arnhem. Thousands of paratroopers had flown in hundreds of Dakotas. He was *sure* he wasn't the only one who had lost a knife, which could have slipped down between the floor and the outside skin of the aircraft. Of all the Dakotas in the world, that particular one could never have chosen to crash in the Nikagwe Hills. And yet . . .

'Where the hell were you thirty-eight bloody years ago?' he said. Then his right stump gave a twinge of pain, from exhaustion or heat or bitter memory he knew not which.

Bert followed in Ako's footsteps through the soaking steamy jungle. He felt the knife in his pocket strike against his thigh with each step of the long trudge home.

As the two men made their way back down the range towards the river, the clouds towering above the Nikagwe hills began to flicker blue tongues of fire and to rumble the news of the impending monsoon. Before Bert and Ako reached the mud-flats the torrential rain was steaming off the warm earth, the broad-leaved trees and their sweat-saturated shirts.

The sudden tropical darkness overtook them, still some miles from the plantation. The voices of the darkened jungle began to swell into the nightly cacophony. The malarial mosquitos, thirsty for blood, started circling the two men.

Bert muttered to himself: 'Great God Almighty! What did I ever do to merit this.'

Chapter 11
TIGER IN THE NIGHT

Once every so often the Clerk of the Weather for the West of Scotland decrees that there is to be a winter day of crystal-clear, perfect flying weather. Light north-easterly winds blow under a flawless blue sky from an Icelandic anticyclone; early morning frost gives way to crisp midday sunshine and tempts skiers up to Glencoe and pilots down to Prestwick or Abbotsinch.

A year or two ago that was just the weather that greeted me at the end of January – the 30th to be exact. It was a Tuesday, but I was due a day off work to compensate for the New Year's Day I had spent, alone with my hangover, in the office. Tuesdays aren't exactly the busiest days for the club's aircraft, so when I got to the airport I had a choice of two Cherokees or an Airtourer; and to minimize the cost of a couple of hours flying, I chose the little 140.

Met confirmed the BBC's forecast; a little morning mist on the east coast, but perfect weather all over the West of Scotland. Great! A whole day free, not a cloud in the sky and a plane with which to share it all. What more could one ask?

Shortly before ten Yankee Papa and I were climbing up, up and away from 06, left turn out and off at 1,500 feet towards the broad waters of the Firth of Clyde, its sea lochs and its islands. One of the attractions of aviating in this area is the almost total freedom of the skies that exists. Outside Scandinavia there's nowhere in Europe to compare with it. North or west of the Scottish TMA there are only a couple of tiny danger areas to avoid, and no worries at all about infringing controlled air space. There are, admittedly, lots of chunks of granite around even as high as FL 44, but that day, as their snowy peaks sparkled and glinted in the sunshine, they merely added to the beauty of the flight, and didn't seem in the least menacing.

My plan, in so far as I'd planned at all, was to go on a solo sightseeing and photographic flight over the islands and, if the Glenforsa strip at Mull was open, to land there for lunch; if not, to get back to Glasgow and sample the dubious delights of the cafeteria in the terminal building there.

Rothesay on the Island of Bute slipped under the nose, and I took a couple of photos as Goat Fell, the highest mountain on Arran, slowly moved past the port wing-tip. The ADF needle swung lazily round, indicating that Skipness NDB was a little to the right and the Mull of Kintyre had been left behind. Out ahead I could see the mountains on the islands of Islay and Jura, peaking 1,000 feet or more above my 1,500-foot cruise; and farther away, a very distant horizon, blue-grey against grey-blue, beyond which I knew lay nothing – nothing but the vast North Atlantic ocean until you reached America. If I followed 56° N right across, I idly mused, where would I make landfall? How did Lindbergh ever cope without even a directional gyro on board and no radio either? Alcock and Brown too? Ah, well, the Cherokee's tanks are small enough to ensure no crazy attempts of that nature today.

I flew between the islands of Islay to the south and Jura to the north, and enjoyed the vicarious thrill of cruising west for a few moments, saying to myself 'Next landfall, the New England coastline!' (On checking up, much later, I was surprised to find that it is Labrador that lies at the same latitude as Scotland. Boston and New York are as far south as Brittany in France.)

To cross-check on my position I tuned in the Tiree VOR, and headed directly towards that most remote of Scottish islands, intending to track back on 095° *from* to have a look-see at Mull and Glenforsa.

I clearly remember peering across the cabin and watching little Colonsay pass under the starboard leading edge; then I decided to switch off the ADF, which was doing nothing but point idly at anything that happened to take its fancy. I wasn't in the mood for any disc jockey's idle chatter that morning. On an impulse, I clicked around the VHF knobs, more or less at random. Scottish FIS had been totally silent – either they had no traffic or maybe I was just in a blind spot – and the speaker merely hissed and crackled a bit, until suddenly a voice broke through the static, and off again as I clicked past the frequency. Out of curiosity I clicked back again: 122.5 – 122.6 – 122.7 – nothing. Or was it the other knob? 122.5 – 123.5 – 124.5. Or the other way? 122.5 – 121.5 and there he was again. Someone way up on the transatlantic airways perhaps, I thought. Then it dawned on me: 121.5 MHz is the distress frequency.

There was an odd timbre to the voice, making it even more difficult to read than the usual chat on a Cherokee lo-fi speaker, and some of the jargon seemed most unfamiliar. 'George', I could hear clearly and then something about being able (or not being able?) and asking how to man something. The 'Mayday' part was clear enough, but then I'd been half expecting that. I waited breathlessly for some ground station to respond, but after a pause of a quarter of a minute or so, the distorted voice came back again. He'd obviously heard no answer either. 'George' was an autopilot, I knew, but if it wasn't able to work I knew nothing about how to help the man; so at the end of the call I again remained silent, keeping my fingers crossed that someone else would reply.

But the next call was the same voice again: 'Mayday Mayday Mayday.' Why doesn't somebody answer, I grumbled to myself, half excited and half scared as it grew more obvious by the minute that I was becoming involved, willy-nilly, in some drama of the air.

I racked my brains back to the RT exam. What is the correct procedure? Don't reply unless no ground station does; just listen out. But no ground station had, so what then? Yes, I remembered, try to act as a relay – making sure the ground station realises it isn't you that is in trouble, but the other aircraft. I couldn't remember any specified form for the message, but with my heart thumping in a ridiculous and unnecessary manner, and the adrenalin level rising rapidly in my bloodstream, I pressed the transmit button and called 'Mayday Mayday Mayday, Scottish Information or other station this is Golf Alfa Victor Yankee Papa. I have intercepted a Mayday call from an unidentified aircraft that received no reply. I am not sure of the nature of his distress but suspect defective autopilot. Golf Yankee Papa Mayday Mayday Mayday over.'

Silence reigned for what seemed an eternity, but was probably ten or fifteen seconds, before the original voice returned to my speaker, a little louder, a little clearer now: 'Mayday Mayday Mayday, George Able How Nan Peter to station relaying my distress call, who are you and what is your present position? Mayday, over.'

I vaguely remembered pulling the leg of an ex-RAF member at the club when he'd relapsed into the 'old' phonetic alphabet once, and I reckoned this pilot must really be in an emergency situation for him to have flipped right back into old habits. My mouth dry with apprehension, I pressed the button again, and forgetting the Mayday this time, tried to sound calm. 'Aircraft in distress. I assume you are Golf Alfa Hotel November Papa. This is PA 140 Golf Alfa Victor Yankee Papa, I am at present 1,500 feet steering 330 towards Tiree Island abeam Colonsay island. Can I assist you? Yankee Papa over'.

'Good morning Yankee Papa . . . ah . . . good to hear from you. We've been trying to raise someone on 121.5 for an hour or so without success . . . ah . . . do not, repeat not, understand your Golf whatsit phonetics or aircraft type but are you equipped to give us any DF or homing assistance, over?'

'Yankee Papa to November Papa sorry negative homing assistance. This is a Cherokee 140 with only VOR and ADF equipment. What is your estimated position? I'll try climbing higher and see if I can relay your Mayday, over.'

I began to feel less panic-stricken and I think I was reacting sensibly. Maintaining my heading towards Tiree I pushed the revs up and trimmed the Cherokee into a 90-knot climb. Surely after three to four minutes I'd be able to raise someone listening out on 121.5 from 3,000 or 4,000 feet up?

Then after a pause, the other aircraft called back: 'George Nan Peter to contact station. We assume you are American aircraft but do not, repeat not, understand your references to Yankees and Cherokees. This is a BSAA flight inbound to the islands and our magnetic and nav instruments seem to be all U/S. We cannot even get an astro fix under the overcast, and up till now we've been able to raise nobody on radio. If you've got a DF can you get a bearing on us, say on . . . ah . . . 500 kay sees or twenty-one eighty-two. First officer is trying to locate these islands names you gave on our map right now, over.'

This guy sounded odd now, in more ways than the metallic quality of the reception. Surely it wasn't a hoax call? How could it be? And what on earth could I do to help? As I passed through 3,500 feet I made another attempt to relay the Mayday on 121.5, then tried Scottish FIS and even Glasgow Approach frequencies, but all was silent. There seemed to be only 'George' and me in or on the air that morning. As I made these abortive calls I realised I could get my ADF set to read 500 kHz, but whether or not that related to 'George's' 500 kay sees I wasn't sure. However, I switched the set back on, clicked in five zero zero, switched back the VHF to 121.5, and in as professional manner as I could muster, spoke again:

'Yankee Papa to . . . ah . . . George (I'd begun to think of my contact as 'George' now, and it came automatically to me as a call sign for him). 'I've been trying again to relay your Mayday on several local frequencies but getting no response, I am uncertain of whether I can get a bearing on you but I've set my ADF to 500 so if you transmit I'll advise you if it responds, over.'

'Roger, Yank, Wilco. Transmitting now continuous carrier wave on 500 kay sees. Have you got any bearing on me? Over.'

With that the ADF needle suddenly ceased its idle wavering and swung purposefully round to point to about 310°. Before getting too excited about it, I pressed the test button, and watched the needle back off, then return positively to the same point when I released it.

'Yankee Papa reporting he appears to have a bearing on you. To confirm, please discontinue transmission for one-five seconds, then resume, over.'

'Roger, ah . . . Yankee. Switching off . . . ah . . . now, over.' I pressed the *test* again, and on releasing it the needle flickered lazily around the 040°-050° area. This was getting exciting again.

'Yankee Papa to George' (not even a hesitation this time), 'Recommence transmission for DF now, over,' and immediately the ADF swung back to indicate 310°. So 'George' was out there somewhere. I looked over to the left, over to the vast expanse of Atlantic, unbroken by any friendly little dots of island, over towards the horizon, and suddenly realised that the blue of the sea and sparkle of the sun in the azure sky had changed. It was as though I was wearing very dark sunglasses. I levelled out, at about 5,000 feet as far as I recall, and watched the sky darken further, with a feeling of real apprehension.

Suddenly George spoke again. 'Can you confirm you have a bearing on me? If so, I propose to orbit my present position, to permit you to fly out to rendezvous and guide me in to the islands. I've got around two to two and a half hours fuel and we can't be all that far out. Can you assist in this way? Over.'

'Yankee Papa confirms a good bearing on you. All you require is to steer a course of around 080° to 100° and you're bound to see the islands soon.' I hated the idea of flying out into the now almost dark vasts of the ocean. 'Can you comply with this suggestion? Over.'

'Negative Yank, sorry. The compasses are all pointing in different directions, the gyros are out and we . . . ah . . . we are unable to steer any given course. I'm commencing to orbit now at 2,000 feet, all nav lights, cabin lights and landing lights on. Let's know when you spot us, over.'

I swallowed hard. 'Roger' I heard my dried-up mouth reply. 'I'm setting course for you now, and switching on my lights too, over.'

'Thanks Yank, we're looking out for you.'

I needed the lights too, for it was getting as black as night. Some straggly cloud was just visible below, so I descended again to get underneath it, and guided by the steady pointing finger of the ADF needle, glowing in the instrument lights, I winged my way on this weird mission, further and further from Scotland, nearer and nearer to what?

I peered into the gloom ahead, level now at just under 2,500 feet. Not a light to be seen. Time dragged past, the Lycoming ran steadily, the ADF needles never flickered from 0°. 'George' must be right up there ahead of me, but how far? Suddenly I remembered *fuel*, and glanced at the gauges. The starboard tank was full, untouched since refuelling at Glasgow, and the port gauge indicated a reading remarkably near the *full* end of the scale, considering the time I'd been in the air. Might as well balance the tanks, I thought, so on with the electric pump, change the selector from port to starboard and off with the pump again. Fuel pressure still okay. Engine still smooth. How long had I been in the air anyway, I asked myself? Take-off had been at 0956, as noted on my pad, and it was now . . . dammit, my watch had stopped at 1041. Must have forgotten to wind it. What about the aircraft clock? It read 1041 also, and the sweep second hand, like that of my wristwatch, was stationary. Curiouser and curiouser, I thought, like the White Rabbit. (He had problems with his watch too!) The engine hourmeter wasn't running either, I discovered, after watching it for some time. Well, at least I had one full fuel tank, and could go on out to sea a bit longer, with plenty of juice to get back to one of the island airfields certainly, even if not to Glasgow.

I had three main worries now. No one knew I was out over the ocean there, and I couldn't tell anyone – except George, and he didn't seem to be in a position to do much to help if anything else more vital that the clock decided to stop! The second worry was what had happened to the daylight? Although I knew I'd flown much more than 45 minutes by now, it certainly shouldn't be getting anywhere near dusk, even in Scottish latitudes where the sun sets at around 1600 in January. And thirdly, who or what was I heading to meet out there?

The Lycoming purred on and on, and the Cherokee flew on very smoothly under the overcast, but my eyes ached as I peered ahead into the gloom to try to distinguish something: not a star, not a light on a ship below, and certainly no sign of aircraft lights.

I felt another twenty minutes or so had passed, with nothing more to mark their passage than two calls and replies between George and myself confirming I still had a bearing and he was still circling and watching. My fuel state looked incredibly healthy too, with the port needle still on the *full* mark. 'They never were all that reliable, these gauges,' I thought. 'Maybe I'd better play safe and not get too much farther away from land. I'll risk another five minutes, or maybe ten, then – but how can I tell when this "limit" is up?' Despite rewinding, my watch was still at a standstill.

Then, quite unexpectedly, the decision was made for me, George's voice crackled through the speaker. 'Hallo Yankee, we've just got you in sight. When we complete this 360 we'll head towards you, and once you've spotted our lights I suggest you make a 180 and lead us home, over.' One could feel the relief in the voice.

Out ahead, a little below a tiny necklace of lights gleamed over the darkness of the ocean, then two brighter stars shone steadily. That must be the cabin lights disappearing as he turns his landing lights towards me to follow, I reasoned, and called 'Commencing 180° turn now' and began to head back towards Scotland. My eyes moved from the ADF to the gyro compass, and to my horror I found it indicated no turn at all. The turn and slip needle, and ball too both remained centred, and – worst of all – the little magnetic compass ball still was reading a steady 270°, although I was more than half-way round my 180 turn. Gyros and compasses out . . . that had an all too familiar sound to it. I stopped the turn when the ADF on 180°

indicated George was now right behind me. At least I knew I had started off in the right direction, but could I steer a straight course in this darkness, without a compass or any landmarks? I doubted it, and doubted it very much indeed. Talk about the blind leading the blind!

Steady now, I told myself. Just keep the plane trimmed nicely in the cruise and she'll fly you straight home herself. Or nearly straight anyway. But would nearly straight be near enough to let me spot Barra or Mingulay or Mull, or would it merely let me lead poor George in a sweeping circle around the North Atlantic? Even a rate one-quarter turn, which is scarcely noticeable in the horizonless dark, means a complete circle every eight minutes. I must do better than this, I told myself, and it came to me in a flash: Tiree VOR, of course! Click click to 112.7 but the flag remained *off*, and the needle didn't budge out of centre at all. No idents could be heard. It was the same story exactly when I turned to Islay, and then Machrihanish, then Prestwick then Glasgow. Every VOR was dead, off the air, silent. I felt very lonely, and not a little scared.

As if sensing my loneliness George spoke to me again. 'Hello Yankee, we've got you clearly in sight now, about half a mile ahead and above us. We're closing fast, so you can increase to normal cruise now, over.'

'Yankee Papa is already at normal cruise' I answered, feeling unjustifiably insulted for some reason.

'Roger, understood' came the response. 'We are dropping wheels and flaps to keep station on your port beam. What type of aircraft are you? Over.'

'Yankee Papa is a PA 28 repeat PA28 . . . a Cherokee 140, over.'

'Ah . . . Roger' with a dubious tone to the voice, 'Is that a twin or a seaplane or what?'

'Yankee Papa is a Charlie-Hotel-Echo-Romeo-Oscar-Kilo-Echo-Echo, single-engined landplane,' I replied.

'Getting a lot of echo in that last transmission,' chuckled George's voice. 'But it's not important. We'll be coming up alongside in about one minute.' He was obviously feeling a lot more relaxed now than when we first spoke to each other.

I returned to the problem of how to steer a straight course, peering at the dark horizon ahead and praying fervently for the outline of an island to appear as an aiming point for me. Discarding the VOR as useless, I fiddled with the ADF for a bit, trying instead

of 500 the 385 of Skipness, then 292 for Barra Head and even 308 for
Tory Island off the Irish coast, but the needle didn't respond to any
one of them, and no signal sounded from the speaker, only mush.
As a last resort I clicked the knobs to tune in the UK's most powerful
'NDB' – the BBC Droitwich transmitter that beamed Radio 2 out on
200 kHz. Even that didn't move the needle or bring a sound to the
speaker. I hadn't a clue as to how to keep the Cherokee straight, or
even whether I was still heading east towards home or perhaps
north towards a watery grave half way to Iceland.

Just then George arrived, nosing into position on my left,
obviously placing full faith and confidence in my ability to lead him
home to safety. Out of the corner of my eye I saw the glow of four
sets of exhaust stacks and a thick Lancaster-type wing, a darkened
cockpit and a row of lighted cabin windows. I picked up my camera
to record the occasion and snapped a couple of photos of my strange
companion. I couldn't at first make out the airline name that was
painted on the fuselage, until I suddenly saw the registration letters
and realised that they were, like the printing of the name, all
reversed as in a mirror's image!

'Hi Yankee!' said the speaker suddenly. 'That's a smart little
aircraft you've got there, even if it is a trifle slow.' I glanced
nervously sideways at the barn-door flaps below the wings and the
enormous bulbous tyres below the inboard engines, which testified
to the pilot's efforts to hold his charge down to my pace. I looked
again at the reversed lettering *G-AHNP* it read. The airline lettering,
once I got it mentally transcribed, read *British South American
Airways*. All the cabin windows were lit, and as my mysterious
companion formated a little closer still, I realised that not a single
face was looking out of any window. No one was to be seen. As the
big plane rocked slightly the cockpit windows too were lit momentarily by a navigation or landing light on the other side, and
silhouetted against the light was the window frame, but no pilot, no
co-pilot, no one at all.

I picked up the mike and pressed the transmit button with a
shaky hand: 'Yankee Papa to November Papa, do you read? Over.'
My voice was quaking as much as my hand was shaking.

The answer was silence.

I repeated the call, adding, for good measure, 'Is there anybody
there? Over.'

Then simultaneously everything began to happen at once. As I watched, my formating neighbour slowly began to lose definition, as though in a heat-haze. The huge single fin and rudder seemed to be made of some soft plastic, and the sharp outline of the fuselage became fuzzy. The cabin lights appeared to go out of focus, and before my eyes the whole aircraft melted into thin air. The last thing I was conscious of seeing was a name painted under the cockpit: *REGIT RATS* it seemed to read, and I can still see it today in its reversed lettering.

Jumbled noises began to emanate from the speaker, as the inane chatter from Waggoner's Walk was trying to submerge a peremptory voice asking 'Station calling on 121.5 please pass your message. Over' and behind it all was the 'dah-ditdit-didahdit' from Tiree confirming which station the *to* flag on the VOR was referring to.

For the life of me I couldn't think of a sensible or suitable or even plausible reply to give to the voice on 121.5, so like a coward I returned to Scottish FIS and kept mum. By the time all this had taken place I found myself back in the bright sunshine of that glorious January day that had been swallowed up, as it seemed, hours ago.

My watch was running again, and agreed with the now-revived aircraft clock that it was now just 1045. I tuned the ADF to Tory Island and found I was almost due north of it, steering 250° directly towards Tiree. That put me at least 130nm from Glasgow, and I'd been flying back east for quite a time in company with the big aircraft – or had I? Time since take-off was apparently only fifty minutes, and winds were light, so the Cherokee must have been averaging over 155 knots even without allowing for the detours around the islands, which I knew I had made and the rescue operation over the Atlantic which, too, I'm sure I made; or had I?

My fuel state looked good still – impossibly good in fact; but for some reason I didn't seem to have much of an appetite, so I routed direct back to Glasgow from Tiree, landed back on 06 and taxied 'YP reflectively back to the club.

I have to admit that isn't a flight I've talked about to anyone since. Especially not since I confirmed my suspicions by looking up a reference book on British airlines and satisfied myself from a couple of photographs in it that my Atlantic companion 'George' couldn't have been anything other than an Avro Tudor; and that *Star Tiger*, a Tudor IV registered G-AHNP, had vanished in the infamous Bermuda Triangle on a flight from the Azores to the Island of

Bermuda on the 30th January 1948, exactly a quarter of a century earlier.

Is there a space or time warp in the Triangle? Of course there isn't; it's simply not possible scientifically to explain or to accept such a thing. But if there isn't a space warp, how could a perfect mirror-image replica of the ill-fated BSAA Tudor IV, complete to its name-lettering REGIT RATS suddenly appear after a series of distress calls, looking for 'the islands' in the mirror-image corner of the North Atlantic? And, without a time warp or something like it, how could I have got to where I was in a conventional Cherokee, with all clocks stopped, gyros U/S and radio aids dead, in pitch darkness on a sunny January morning?

I can't explain it either, nor can I even prove it ever happened, unless you'll accept as evidence an uncut strip of 35 mm colour film with four nicely exposed aerial views of Scottish islands, then two frames of utter blackness followed by a series of snaps of my daughter's birthday party on the 5th of February. I realise that doesn't prove much, but I shall confide in you on one other point: almost a year later, on 17th January, my log book, quite deliberately and according to plan, shows I did no flying at all. That's because my reference books told me that *Star Tiger's* sister plane G-AGRE, the BSAA Tudor IV *Star Ariel*, also vanished twenty-five years earlier on that date en route from Bermuda to Jamica; and if her ghostly mirror-image was searching for an island off the West Coast of Scotland that day, I'm afraid I decided I simply didn't want to get involved.

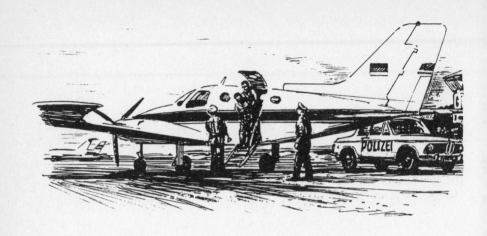

Chapter 12
UNNATURAL CAUSES

Hans-Werner Lechner was never the most popular member of the flying club at Rösingen. In fact he never enjoyed much popularity anywhere, in all of the twenty-eight years he had lived in and around the little industrial town on the edge of Germany's beautiful Black Forest region.

He hadn't even been much of a success as a bully while at school near Stuttgart, nor as a scholar either, and when he returned to Rösingen without the qualifications for university entrance his popularity with his factory manager father Willi Lechner reached a pretty low ebb, too.

Hans-Werner settled into an uninspired but none too unpleasant way of life, working half-heartedly in the sales office of the Lechner family textile business. He expected, as the only son, to take over the business in the fullness of time, and meantime enjoyed spending his fairly generous salary on good wine, on women of more questionable quality and on flying.

Rösingen airfield is on the other side of town from the Lechner factory. It is perched, like so many small German airfields, astride a ridge of rolling hill country. From the air it looks like a pale emerald stripe amongst the dark-green slopes of conifer-clad hills on three sides, and the red-tile roofs of the town on the fourth. The airfield, with the clubhouse, the miniature control tower and two little fuel pumps beside the hangar had been there since Hans-Werner was a child, but it wasn't until he'd reached his twenties that he ever really noticed it.

And when he did, it was only because a current girlfriend had teased him about his lack of enthusiasm for motorbikes.

'My last boyfriend used to take me pillion on his BMW and we'd do 180 on it. Brought the tears to your eyes, and it could get you really turned-on too', she told him.'

'Kids' stuff, that', he'd retorted. 'When he grows up, he'll grow out of it.' Hans-Werner smiled, a little smugly.

'God, I do believe I've got it,' said the girl. 'You're scared of bikes, scared of speed. The great Hans-Werner Lechner's chicken.' She burst out laughing.

Hans-Werner was furious and before he knew what he was saying he'd asserted, 'Rubbish; I get my thrills from something a lot more dangerous and faster than a bloody BMW bike. I'm a pilot. Do aerobatics as a hobby. No time to waste on bikes.'

It was the look that appeared in her eyes that did it. The sparkle that had accompanied her derisive laughter changed character almost imperceptibly as her eyes narrowed in suspicion. Then it grew into a warm glow as they widened again. She'd swallowed the story.

On his way home later that night Hans-Werner mused to himself that if the mere idea of aerobatic flight could do that to one female, what on earth would the real thing do to others?

Six months later he found himself a few thousand marks poorer, but richer by one pilot's licence, over fifty flying hours and the sure knowledge that aerobatics just made him miserably ill.

Still the BMW bike girl had disappeared (back to her BMW boy-friend for all Hans-Werner cared), having unwittingly acted as the catalyst to start the reaction between young Lechner and aviation. And once Reinhard Kruger, the CFI at Rösingen started allowing him to fly with passengers in the club's Cessna 172, Hans-Werner made the discovery that even straightforward amateur flying turned some of his current paramours on, too. He decided to forget all about aerobatics, and to concentrate on more or less horizontal activities with his metal birds as well as his other ones.

Once he got round to buying his own areoplane, a brand new, fully IFR-equipped Piper Archer, his rather limited popularity with other club members seemed to increase. More people were willing at least to put up with his company in order to have the occasional opportunity of flying his aircraft, the best-equipped in the club's fleet.

Things could have gone on like that for some time but for the coincidence of Herr Willi Lechner falling out violently with his son the very week Hans-Werner had signed a purchase order for a twin-engineed Beechcraft to replace the Archer.

The Lechner family argument had been slowly coming to a head. Lack of application to his job and lack of interest in the family firm were the main complaints his father levelled against Hans-Werner, but as the argument hotted up, it spread into other fields. His spendthrift habits, his expensive taste in wine, his cheap taste in women and above all his ridiculously time and money consuming, utterly useless hobby of flying were all cited against him. Finally Hans-Werner found himself out of the family firm, out of work and almost out of funds.

To make matters worse, he heard via his current girlfriend, who knew his father's private secretary, that his father was having a lawyer draw up papers, putting the firm into a trust and altering his will to exclude Hans-Werner entirely from any chance of inheriting any share in it. The documents were to be ready for signature the following Monday.

Hans-Werner's first reaction was to disbelieve the news. His second was to tackle his father directly and try to persuade him to change his mind. Then, remembering the impossible take-off position he had for any such argument, he decided to try an entirely different course of action.

He telephoned his mother, ostensibly swallowed his pride and told her he wanted to apologise and explain what he had in mind. After an initial refusal even to see him, old Willi softened under Frau Lechner's persuasion, and Hans-Werner found himself that Friday evening at the family dinner-table again.

The atmosphere was decidedly strained. Each time Hans-Werner tried to steer the desultory conversation in the direction he wanted, his father ignored him and changed the subject. Finally, with dinner finished, Herr Lechner senior nodded to his wife who discreetly left father and son together for their *tête à tête*.

'You've something on your mind, Hans-Werner. Let's hear about it now.'

Carefully striving to avoid any hint that he knew anything about the impending change in his prospects of inheriting the family business, Hans-Werner set about convincing his father of his intentions to prove himself a competent businessman in the field of his own choosing, aviation. Possibly unable to avoid a guilty feeling concerning the papers he was scheduled to sign three days later, Lechner senior gave him a fair hearing. His patience began to wear thin as Hans-Werner got round to talking about finance for the project, then he was suddenly surprised into silence when he was told that the Badische Kredit Bank had agreed to finance the projected aviation business.

'Against my guarantee?' he asked suspiciously.

'No, Father, neither you nor the company is involved. The Bank knows a good thing when it sees one. They realise aircraft aren't just expensive toys, but real investments, with good money-making potential. I wish you'd try to realise that investments in things other than textile machinery can pay off too, Father.'

Herr Lechner still looked dubious. He was sure this meeting had been arranged to try to get his financial support for some hare-brained scheme. But he wasn't being asked for cash, or even a guarantee, so Hans-Werner must somehow have got the Bank to back him. It was difficult to believe.

'There must be something in it, I suppose', he said slowly, half to himself. 'Otherwise the BKB wouldn't be risking their capital.'

'Of course there's something in it', said Hans-Werner. 'They've insisted on all sorts of insurance cover and so on but it's all tied up now. I'm picking up the first of my new aircraft from Stuttgart tomorrow. Look, Father, I'd like to feel you and I were going to get along better now I'm out of your hair in the office, and for that to happen, you've got to try to understand aviation. I'd love to show you something of the pleasure and the business potential of general aviation and convince you that there's more to flying than sitting in the back of an Airbus or a Boeing. Why not fly to Stuttgart with me tomorrow in the Archer, then do me the honour of being my new company's first passenger in the new plane on the way back to Rösingen?'

Mellowed by the wine, in a state of surprise about the bank loan, disoriented by not having been pressed by Hans-Werner for money, old Herr Lechner was off guard. Before he'd realised it, he had agreed to fly the short return journey to Stuttgart with his son next day.

Not wishing to worry Frau Lechner about his going flying, all he told his wife after Hans-Werner had left that evening, was that he'd agreed to see their son on Saturday 'about what he's planning to do, now he's left the business'.

Which was true, as far as it went.

Saturday was a fine day for flying, with a few scattered cumulus about 3,000 feet and good visibility all over the Black Forest area.

'Not a bad day', mused Herr Willi Lechner on his way to the airfield, 'for a stupid old man of sixty-six with high blood pressure to go up in a stupid little aeroplane for the first time.' He was nervous, but certainly unwilling to lose face, having agreed to make the journey. He parked at the airfield, and popped a couple of little pink pills into his mouth. They always helped remove the incipient headache he felt when he got tense, and they worked again this time.

Hans-Werner strode across the grass in his direction. He looked pleased to see his father, pleased as well as relieved. He'd been afraid his father would change his mind overnight, or telephone the manager of the bank and expose the story of the loan and the new business as the hoax it all was. However, all now seemed set for stage two of his scheme.

'Nice to see you', he called across. 'And you've brought some lovely flying weather with you, too.'

'It is all right, is it?' answered the older man, with a slightly apprehensive look at the almost cloudless sky. Deep down he wished it had turned out to be thick fog that Saturday morning. Still, he'd never been known to back out of anything once he'd given his word, and he certainly wasn't going to start doing so now, with Hans-Werner as a witness.

The two Lechners walked across to the Piper Archer. Hans-Werner opened the door, scrambled across to the left-hand seat and watched his father as he pulled himself, slightly out of breath, into the front passenger seat. Hans-Werner leaned across, slammed the door, locked it, then juggled a few switches and knobs to bring the engine to life.

'All set, Father?' he asked, lined up for take-off on the grass runway.

The old man, looking older than usual, nodded, swallowed hard, and tried unsuccessfully to look unconcerned.

'It's a lot smoother once we're in the air', Hans-Werner called across the cabin, as the Archer bumped and shuddered, accelerating along the rough grass strip.

His father nodded once again.

'There!' Hans-Werner cried. 'I told you, didn't I?' as the plane climbed over the fir trees, banked and swung round to cross the little town at about 1,000 feet.

'Look Father', he said. 'There's our factory down there on your side. See it?'

Herr Lechner found his voice sufficiently to say 'Yes, Hans-Werner, I can see my factory quite plainly.' There was an emphasis on the word 'my' that caused Hans-Werner's knuckles to whiten slightly on the control yoke and his stomach muscles to tighten, as he remembered the end-purpose of the mission he was now flying. Trying to keep his voice normal, he said, 'If you're feeling as tense as you sound, Father, why not have a cigarette? Relax and enjoy the scenery. Smoking's allowed in the cockpit.'

He pulled out a pack of Marlboro and said, 'Try one of these. They're quite mild.'

'Shouldn't really. Doctor's orders, you know.'

'One will do you more good than harm. Relax you. Ease the blood pressure.'

'I don't believe the latter part, but I'll risk one.'

As father and son sat together, smoking quietly, the Archer, still at climbing power, continued to put more fresh air between itself and the wooded hills of the rolling green landscape.

Herr Lechner had regained a little colour, and seemed more composed as he stubbed out his cigarette and peered around him. They were now over 5,000 feet above the ground.

'Where exactly are we, Hans-Werner?'

'There's the Rhine over on my side', Hans-Werner pointed, 'With the Vosges mountains in France beyond. Freiburg's over there and . . . wait a minute', he pulled the Archer round 180° in a sudden rate three turn.

'There are the Alps in Switzerland.'

Row upon row of gleaming white mountains paralleled the southern horizon, with the sun reflecting from their eternal glaciers. It was a breathtaking panorama, but it was the sudden turn and not the snowy tops that had taken Herr Willi Lechner's breath away. Looking a little grey again, he said, tetchily, 'Yes, yes, Hans-Werner, magnificent, but can't you try to make this thing turn a little more gently next time?'

Meekly Hans-Werner brought the Archer slowly round towards a more northerly heading again. Relentlessly the engine blattered away at climbing power, and the altimeter needles rotated steadily past the 9,000 feet indication. Hans-Werner tuned in the No. 1 VOR set to pick up a beacon, situated under busy Airway Amber 9 that leads the airliners from Frankfurt to Zurich. He was keeping well to the west of that. Didn't want to have any near-misses with IFR traffic, although he *was* going to risk penetrating the permanent VFR restricted area that covers all Germany above Flight Level 100.

He let the nose swing slowly west, and then south without arousing any suspicions in his father's mind.

Even with the throttle open fully, the Archer was climbing more slowly now in the thinner air, but they had passed the 12,000 feet mark, and Hans-Werner began to notice what he'd been waiting for. His father's reactions to the remarks he was making were slower, and his speech slightly slurred. He had lost what little interest he'd ever had in the flight and was sitting slouched against his harness and the cockpit door. The lack of oxygen in the thin high-altitude air was combining with his circulatory weakness to produce a semi-coma.

Hans-Werner eased the throttle back slightly and trimmed the Archer into level flight.

'Wha'ch zat?' said his father, looking up as the noise level altered.

'Nothing of importance', snapped Hans-Werner aggressively. 'But now listen, for I have something of importance to say to you. Can you hear me?'

"F course I c'n hear you', replied his father, unconvincingly.

Hans-Werner shook him by the shoulder. The older man reacted to this unaccustomed treatment by wakening up momentarily from his state of anoxia.

'Wha' d'you mean . . .' he began indignantly but his son interrupted him abruptly.

'Listen to me you evil, tyrannical, self-opinionated bastard that I've been blessed with as a father. You never liked me, from the day I was born. You hated me, but still wanted me to be your bloody lap-dog. Do this, don't do that. Criticism, blame, complaints, that's all I've ever had from you. And now, you sneaky shyster, you're planning to steal my very inheritance behind my back.'

His voice was halfway between a scream and a snarl, his eyes, bright and staring, never left his father's for an instant. The aircraft flew in a gentle curve high above the Rhine.

'Yes, I know all about your bloody scheming against me', he continued. Herr Lechner's eyes stared back dull in contrast to the maniacal gleam in his son's. He tried to speak.

'No! Shut your mouth', snapped Hans-Werner. 'You've done all the talking all your bossy little life. Now you're going to do the listening for what little is left of it. For, get this straight. You aren't going to sign these papers on Monday. No way! And d'you know why? Simply because you aren't getting out of this aeroplane alive. That's why!'

His father's breathing was becoming shallow again, and faster. His eyes, wide with fear, looked glazed, his face pale.

'And there won't be a mark on your miserable body', continued Hans-Werner. 'Natural causes, that's what the verdict will be.' He began to laugh loudly, drowning the sound of the engine, and of his father's gasps for breath.

'Natural causes', he repeated gleefully. 'And while you're dying of natural causes, just think how much pleasure I'm going to get when they read your will and I inherit the business despite your nasty little game to cheat me, you bloody hypocrite! But I wasn't born yesterday. You're not clever enough for me, see! Just think about that while you're breathing your last. You signed your own death warrant when you drafted your new will. Cunning you were, but not cunning enough for me!' he cried in a cackle of triumph, watching the bewildered, helpless look on the old man's face.

Suddenly he thumped the throttle wide open again, pushed the Archer's nose down to gather speed, and then pulled the aircraft into a viciously tight right-hand turn. He braced every muscle in his body, then wound the turn tighter until his feet felt like lead as the g-forces built up. His father slouched in the seat beside him, gasping for breath, his face devoid of colour. His vision became a blur of greys, then black. He couldn't lift his arms. His head lolled forward.

Hans-Werner eased the Archer out of the turn, and looked. The figure in the right-hand seat began to move again. It raised its head, and turned with a pleading look towards him. Hans-Werner grinned evilly at it and began applying g again as he went from level flight into a rate four turn. He began to notice he was greying out himself, and decided he'd better get down a couple of thousand feet before he passed out, too. The descent was a screamingly tight spiral, wings almost vertical as the Archer corkscrewed its way towards slightly denser air below.

Herr Lechner knew nothing of this. His terror had pushed his blood pressure up to intolerable levels, the effects of nicotine, anoxia and g-forces which made his blood three times heavier than normal, were all too much for his heart. Before they had descended through 10,000 feet his heart-beat, already over-rapid, had become a frenzied flutter and then ceased altogether.

Back in straight and level flight Hans-Werner watched his passenger to see if he regained consciousness but there was no sign of movement. To check if his father was merely playing possum he abruptly closed the throttle and kicked the rudder to skid the aircraft. The body beside him only slouched further against the cockpit door. There was no other reaction to the sudden change in noise level and movement. Hans-Werner leaned across to feel his father's wrist. There was no pulse.

But he had to be sure. So he used the mirror he'd brought with him, to make certain all breathing had stopped. He was now positive there was no fear of his father's recovering as he went in to land. He'd accomplished what he'd planned.

He picked up the microphone, dialled in 118.25 MHz on his radio and contacted Freiburg airfield.

'Mayday, Mayday, Mayday.' He called the international distress call. He explained who he was, where he was, and that his passenger had become unconscious and seemed in need of medical attention.

'I'm diverting to your field instead of Stuttgart', he told Freiburg, 'since you're closer. Can you have an ambulance or a helicopter there to meet me, please? My ETA with you is in about ten minutes.'

'Roger, we'll do what we can. The runway is 16 and you will be number one to land in three minutes from now.'

An ambulance with a doctor met Hans-Werner at the 34 end of the runway. As they transferred Herr Lechner's body from the Archer, the doctor shook his head and said to the pilot.

'Sorry old chap, I'm afraid there's nothing we can do for your passenger. Was he a personal friend of yours?'

'My Father', said Hans-Werner, and burst into tears. The doctor wasn't to know they were tears of relief.

The post-mortem, inquest and issue of Herr Lechner's death certificate all went in a straightforward and routine manner. The formalities were necessary in view of the circumstances of the death. Hans-Werner's evidence that his father, after apparently enjoying the first half-hour of his flight had become unwell and then collapsed was accepted without reserve or query. After all, the post-mortem evidence showed a simple heart-attack, an event that couldn't be regarded as unexpected in a man of Herr Willi Lechner's age, and with his medical history.

The widowed Frau Lechner expressed her annoyance at Hans-Werner for having persuaded his father to fly, but Hans-Werner was feigning such grief that she felt he was too upset to pursue the matter.

Hans-Werner then returned to the Lechner factory, this time to the office that had been his father's. He had enough sense to delegate most of the decision-making to others with more experience in textiles than he.

He embezzled enough company money to complete the deal to buy his twin, and soon began enjoying his favourite life style, his wine, his travel and his women in a more expansive way than ever.

He was blissfully unaware of the growing interest that Kommissaris Klaus Ziegler of the Freiburg police criminal division was taking in his activities.

A chance meeting at a businessmen's dinner had brought Kommissaris Ziegler into conversation with the late Herr Lechner's lawyer. In the course of their conversation the lawyer had mentioned how lucky Hans-Werner Lechner had been that his father had died that day, and not forty-eight hours later, when it would all have been a very different story for him. Ziegler's professional nose twitched, his interest was aroused and he decided to look into this apparently fortuitous coincidence.

Early in his investigations Ziegler engineered a social meeting with Hans-Werner, and disliked him instinctively. He managed to suppress this feeling sufficiently to feign an interest in the Lechner textile business and Hans-Werner invited him to visit the Rösingen factory. Ziegler drew up a list of names of employees who could have known about Lechner senior's intentions concerning his son, or about the document his lawyer had prepared for Lechner's signature.

He soon eliminated most of these, and finally came to the conclusion that the planning of the changes had been done so secretly that only Willi Lechner, his private secretary and the lawyer could have known anything, prior to the fatal flight. The girl made no secret of her dislike of Hans-Werner, and had in fact left the Lechner business almost as soon as he had taken over as boss. She certainly had not warned him of the impending change.

The circumstances reeked of suspicion to Ziegler's police-trained mind, but he could find no evidence to corroborate these suspicions.

He rechecked the medical reports, and found them sufficiently conclusive to make any request for exhumation futile. The body bore no marks of violence, and forensic tests had revealed the presence of Lechner's normal medication in his stomach and bloodstream, with no trace of any other drugs or poison.

Ziegler maintained his acquaintance with Hans-Werner, gradually becoming more and more convinced that the old man's death had been foul play. After a club dinner one evening an inebriated Hans-Werner bragged that he knew why Ziegler was hanging around him, but he was wasting his time. Even if Ziegler could prove he had known anything about the unsigned document he couldn't do a bloody thing about it, because his father had died of natural causes and they had medical certificates to prove it.

Ziegler was not a man to give up easily. He was determined to find out just what part Hans-Werner had played in his father's death. The question was . . . how?

Finally the Kommissaris decided to resort to an old police technique: reconstruction of the crime. It wasn't an easy task. If crime there had been, it had taken place somewhere in the skies high above the Black Forest. He enlisted the help of the CFI of the Rösingen Flying Club, with whom Hans-Werner had never been particularly popular, and also of Günther Fichtel, whose name was better known in theatrical than in police or aviation circles. He was an adept impersonator and mimic, about the same build as Willi Lechner had been, and could imitate his slight Swabian accent beautifully.

He also enlisted the help of Hans-Werner's own vanity and boastfulness.

'The police department is trying to decide whether to buy a helicopter or a twin for traffic duties, and one of the types under consideration is a Cessna 402. Since you and Kruger from the flying club are the only two really independent people I know who've got twin ratings and whose opinions I'd trust, I wonder if you'd help me by doing a flight appraisal for me next week?'

Hans-Werner was flattered.

'We won't really need old Kruger along, but I suppose if you want, he can go for the ride. I'll be delighted to help.'

'We'll have another two policemen along from the traffic department. Okay by you?'

"Course it's okay. You're paying the bill, you can pick the passengers.'

Günther Fichtel, furnished with the background to the affair and some photographs of the deceased Herr Lechner, had been briefed to arrive at the airfield an hour before the scheduled take-off time, and to install himself behind the curtain that concealed a little toilet area at the rear of the cabin. Twenty minutes after take-off he was to begin his act.

The three policemen and two pilots assembled on time and went out to board the aircraft.

'I've done the pre-flight', Kruger informed Hans-Werner, who, never greatly interested in such formalities, contented himself with a quick external walk round before settling himself into the left-hand seat.

'All set then?' he queried, before firing up the two powerful Continental engines, and taxying out.

They took off, and climbed uneventfully towards the north, over the undulating landscape of the tree-covered hills of the Black Forest, with the River Rhine visible to their left, beyond the port engine-nacelle and wing.

'You okay for a few moments?' Kruger asked Hans-Werner.

'Of course. Why?'

'I'd like to see how this thing feels from the passenger's point of view. I think I'll go aft and sit beside Ziegler for a little.'

'Please yourself then', said Hans-Werner.

Kruger slipped out of the right-hand seat and went back to the first row of passenger seats. Hans-Werner concentrated on retuning some of the avionics and trying to identify some of the instrumentation, more complex than he was accustomed to. The Cessna 402 droned on steadily.

'Check out the autopilot', Kruger called to him.

'Okay; just a minute', answered Hans-Werner, fumbling for the appropriate switches. There was a slight clunk as the autopilot engaged.

'There', he said. 'That's it.'

He was gazing out across the Rhine Valley and didn't notice the curtain by the toilet move aside. The figure of an elderly man slid softly forward between the passenger seats and sat down in the right-hand pilot's position.

'Back already?' said Hans-Werner, without looking round.

On getting no reply he glanced to his right, froze rigid and gasped.

'God Almighty! What the hell?'

White-faced, he slowly turned round to look at his passengers. Kruger, Ziegler and the two other policemen were sitting quite unconcerned, behind him.

'What did you say? queried Ziegler.

'What the hell's *he* doing here? What's going on?' cried Hans-Werner.

'What d'you mean? said Ziegler, innocently. 'What's *who* doing where?'

Hans-Werner ignored him. He turned to the figure in the seat beside him.

'You can't be here. You're dead, you old bastard. Dead, dead, dead!'

'Who the hell are you talking to?'

'Him, there, of course. Don't you see?' Hans-Werner looked to his right.

'Kruger's back here', said Ziegler. 'There's only the four of us here, plus you. What are you playing at?'

All his passengers assumed expressions of blank bewilderment at their pilot's behaviour. Hans-Werner began to scream.

'Are you all blind? He's there! Can't you see?'

'Yes, Hans-Werner, I'm here. Just the way I was here a month or two ago, with you in another aircraft, wasn't I? Remember? Remember you told me how you hated me then? You told me you knew all about the changes I was going to make to my will. Then you told me I'd never live to sign the papers. I'd be dead before you landed.'

He was playing the part magnificently, better even than Ziegler had ever dared to hope. Hans-Werner was as white as a sheet, while the Cessna droned on under autopilot. Then he began pounding his thighs with his clenched fists, his head bowed.

'And you *were* dead too. I'm *sure* you were. I checked your pulse, and your breathing. You *must* have been dead. I took you up so high you nearly died of anoxia even before I pulled the tight turns to finish you off. I killed you. I know I did. You can't be . . . you can't . . .'

He looked right again. The figure had gone. He turned round, horror-struck.

Kruger moved quickly back into the right-hand pilot's seat as Ziegler snapped handcuffs on the wrists behind the still-clenched fists.

The two policemen removed Hans-Werner, blabbering and jabbering incoherently, into the rear of the cabin. Kruger moved across, switched off the autopilot and flew the big Cessna back to Freiburg airfield.

As the two policemen escorted Hans-Werner Lechner away from the aircraft a man came running towards it from the control tower.

'Kommissaris Ziegler', he called. 'I've got a message for you. Telegram arrived just a few minutes after you took off.'

He handed an envelope to Ziegler, standing beside Kruger in the cabin door of the aircraft. He tore it open and read.

'Regret unable to attend for today's performance due to broken leg. Apologies. Günther Fichtel.'

Ziegler turned from the door of the Cessna and jerked back the toilet curtain. The tiny compartment behind was empty.

Chapter 13
THE ANIMAL LOVER

From an early age John Lindsay Swan had always shown a keen interest in birds and animals. By the time he was at school he had a collection of pet rabbits in his parents' garden near the tall, sandy Norfolk cliffs overlooking the North Sea not far from Sheringham. In the cottage itself he kept guinea-pigs and some budgerigars for good measure.

Before he was in his teens John had confided in friends and family that he was going to be a vet. His ambitions never varied over the next few years. He couldn't even bring himself to eat the occasional rabbit his father killed to augment their meagre wartime meat rations. He would rather go to bed hungry. He often found it hard to sleep with his stomach empty and his head full of the roar of aircraft engines as the Allied bomber fleets passed overhead on their way to batter Europe.

The seabirds around the Norfolk coast fascinated John. He would watch them for hours as they wheeled and soared the up-currents along the cliff face. Quite frequently he scrambled down the zig-zag path that led past a tangle of brilliant sunshine-yellow gorse bushes from the family cottage through the sandy cliffs to the beach below, to seek out any birds in need of help. Many were the gulls and guillemots who owed their lives to his cleaning oil from their feathers after the torpedoing of a ship somewhere in the North Sea had caused slicks to drift ashore. He could splint broken wings and legs too, and one of his favourite, though infrequent, outings was the few miles to Blakeney with its throngs of gulls and geese and all manner of waterfowl.

John was called up in 1944 when he was eighteen. He volunteered for the cavalry in the forlorn hope that there might still be some horses somewhere in the background of the mechanised engines of war, but he soon found himself passing some strange aptitude tests and posted in a light-blue uniform to Desford. There at 7 EFTS he began to learn to fly Tiger Moths, the first step on his long journey to the co-pilot's seat of a clumsy-looking old Bristol Freighter.

At the end of his elementary flying training he opted for fighters, but predictably, found himself posted to an Anson-equipped advanced school, on his way to becoming a bomber pilot.

As his brief training period neared its completion, Pilot Officer Swan put his name down for a Lancaster squadron, but then so did almost everyone on the course, so he wasn't really surprised when he ended up stationed on a bleak Lincolnshire airfield where his first operational squadron was equipped with Halifaxes.

Pilot Officer John Swan never completed his first 'tour'. This wasn't for the usual sombre reason, but simply because the war in Europe came to an end after he had flown only seven missions. The second-last of those had been to Dresden, and after reading later of the holocaust he had helped to create of that refugee-crammed city in an already defeated Germany, he spent sleepless nights in the now lethargic officers' mess of the purposeless bomber station.

It wasn't until his log book showed almost a thousand flying hours (many of which had been flown at the controls of Halifaxes converted to carry food and coal instead of bombs) that he felt he had expiated his treatment of Dresden that far-off night, by his efforts in keeping Berlin alive through the exhausting days of the Air Lift.

Then suddenly the RAF and a mature, experienced twenty-two year old Flying Officer Swan parted company. A peace-time air force had no room for him, and if he was honest with himself, John had to admit he really didn't have much time for it, either. He felt he was too old to start veterinary training now, and anyway the civilian aircraft industry and airline networks were building up rapidly.

Exciting new aircraft like the Viking, the DC4, Brabazon, Ambassador and Constellation were thrusting into the skies, to oust the old converted bombers, or pre-war civilian designs like the Dakota. The future for a man with John Lindsay Swan's qualifications and experience was bright.

After fourteen months of intermittent unemployment and menial ground jobs around various airports he finally managed to persuade an embryonic cargo airline to sign him on as second pilot of their Bristol 170 Freighter. He reaccustomed himself to the feel of a flight-deck and the sound of Hercules radials thundering reassuringly on each side of him. Chambers Cargo Airlines prospered, and John Swan prospered too, although not entirely as the result of the second pilot's salary he drew from them.

John had found that useful money-making contacts could be made in and around the various airfields of Europe and North Africa that formed his territory in the early fifties. Chambers Airlines' lumbering old Freighter often carried some odd pieces of unofficial cargo which Mr Chambers knew nothing about and which the customs authorities knew equally little about. John's various captains either knew nothing about it or were prepared to turn a blind eye, since they probably had something similar stowed away somewhere else on board.

John usually tried to make sure that whatever he was smuggling it wasn't drugs. He drew the line at that. Watches and jewels, caviare and nylons, ammunition and blood-plasma, it was amazing to him the diverse articles that people wanted moved quickly and unobtrusively around the world. And it was amazing how generously some of his contacts were prepared to fork out, once he had proved himself to be a reliable courier.

Cargo flying itself didn't offer much in the way of glamour, nor all that much in the way of excitement, compared with the hectic days of the Berlin Air Lift or the adrenalin-stimulating days of threading bombers through the radar screens, night-fighters, searchlights and flak that had been John's experience of the dying throes of the Third Reich.

It did have its moments, though. There were nights when Turin to Britain involved an idyllic flight through star-studded velvety skies with moonlight picking out the icy Alpine peaks below them. Tiny twinkles in the darker hollows between the glaciers betrayed the locations of Swiss mountain hamlets. And other nights when the same journey was a nightmare of turbulence and down-draughts in gale-tossed clouds. Ice fragments from the propellers shattered explosively against the fuselage sides. The broad, ungainly wings of the Freighter became steadily thicker and heavier, as ice built up and threatened to force them down into the frozen granite cliffs waiting hungrily, invisible and not all that far below.

Dust-clouds like evil yellow fungi rose from the fringes of the Sahara and blotted out everything including landing fields. The mistral howled down the Rhone valley, reducing the north-bound Freighter to a ground speed of eighty and finally put its destination, Lyons, beyond the fuel range of the aircraft. That had resulted in a forced landing in Montelimar, and a few awkward moments with a customs official who was convinced the crew had staged it to deliver smuggled cargo there. In fact, the captain had several litre-bottles of essences for perfume manufacture stored in the starboard wing root and John had ten packages of gold-topped Parker 51 pens tucked away behind the cable looms at the side of the forward cargo section. All either man wanted was to get the hell out of Montelimar with as little fuss as possible.

Instrument landing was still in its infancy in the fifties, and when autumnal England drew the customary blankets of fog and mist around its shoulders, the only way back to earth for the Freighter, groaning under its five tons of legal and illicit cargo, was either a GCA or, more usually, a Standard Beam Approach. At the end of a long haul, with the slightly out-of-synch throb of the Hercules singing relentlessly in his ears, there was little John could imagine that was less enjoyable than having to haul the heavy controls of the 170 to force it to fly round the complex pattern of the SBA. His tired ears were assailed constantly by high-pitched morse 'dit-dah' or 'dah-dit' sounds that blended excruciatingly together into a steady squeal in his headphones once he had centred the beast on the approach beam.

Still, he'd been doing it since his days in Ansons. It had once got him safely home into fog-bound Lincolnshire with half his Halifax's port wing-tip and aileron shot away by a Junkers 88 night fighter. He'd lost count of the number of times he'd generated a thumping headache as a result of SBA's during his Berlin days, so another few now wouldn't harm him.

Mink farming was becoming a popular get-rich-quick scheme in Britain, and the ferret-like little animals were beginning to fetch ridiculous prices as breeding stock. One of John's contacts broached the subject with him one night over a few beers. He had heard that mink were still cheap and easy to get hold of in Romania and Bulgaria, but unfortunately Chambers Cargo Airlines' routes didn't extend beyond the Iron Curtain. Not many airlines did at that time.

John made use of another of his contacts, this time in Ankara, and arranged for an unscrupulous boatman in Zonguldak to make contact with Bulgarian fishermen from near Varna at a rendezvous in the Black Sea. As a trial run, a couple of dozen Transylvanian mink were brought across via two boats to Turkey and via the unsuspecting Mr Chambers' Bristol Freighter, to Britain. And, despite the pay-offs to the two boatmen, the Turkish contact and to John, there was still apparently a big enough margin in the deal to make it a worthwhile venture to repeat.

So John repeated it. He had always been fond of animals, and the financial rewards involved made him especially fond of these.

He received the animals in wooden crates with air holes which he covered, for customs inspections, either with 'This side up' or 'Fragile' labels, or duplicates of the labels used on the official cargo packages. Just in case the customs agents did a careful count, John usually managed to alter the numbers on the cargo manifest to correspond with the actual number of crates on board.

It always seemed to work. John busied himself cooking the crew rosters to make sure he was on board every Chambers Cargo Airlines aircraft that was Turkey bound. Each time he could get six crates of the little beasts hidden in the hold, he stood to gain as much as would have bought him a mink-lined flying jacket if his tastes had run in that direction.

He began toying with the idea of actually chartering an aircraft himself and bringing in a whole five tons of the brutes legally. Then he realised he'd no idea whether they should be subject to quarantine, or what import duty would apply, or even whether such a thing as a Turkish export licence for mink existed. He decided, as he did the hard work on a morning approach to Naples airport for a refuelling stop, that things were probably best left just as they were.

Full of fuel, legally loaded Turkish tobacco, and illegally stowed livestock, the Freighter's upward climb from Naples was at a very shallow angle. Vesuvius was almost out of sight behind them before they had even drawn level with its meagre 3,900 feet height. The old girl staggered up slowly through the sky with its gradually increasing layers of stratiform cloud, until it was safe to meander round the westernmost of the Alpine peaks, en route for home. Beyond the Alps all of France was covered in cloud, and to judge from radio met reports, the cloud went uncomfortably close to the ground, forming fog in places.

Normally the little stowaway animals seemed to find their ferry flights pretty dull, individually packaged inside dark crates with wire mesh reinforcement. As the air got thinner and the temperature dropped in the Freighter's hold, most of them seemed to settle down to snooze the journey away. There were exceptions, of course, and some succumbed on the journey, which cut down John's profit. If they died of pneumonia later that was his UK contact's worry.

There was one other exception, and he (or was it she?) was on board this time. Instead of sleeping its way to England this little creature spent the time from Ankara to Naples worrying at a loose bit of wire with its vicious little teeth. Ultimately the wire snapped and it began to claw and scratch and bite the wood of the crate beyond. Somewhere around Rome its teeth finally got through the last strands of wood fibre and it rapidly clawed a hole, just big enough to slip through.

Out of one dark cold metallic box into another similar, if bigger one. It scuttled down the cold slippery aluminium floor of the aircraft, between the bales and boxes of tobacco, towards the tail of the Freighter. It was oblivious of the fact that it was now passing right overhead the island of Elba.

By the time the Alps were lying a hundred nautical miles behind, the mink had found a slightly warmer place, just behind the cabin bulkhead, where a little of the heated cabin air escaped as a warm draft into the hold. It scuttled and scrambled around the metal stringers running lengthwise down the fuselage sides and discovered a snug perch where the electrical cable loom came through the bulkhead, and where more warm air flowed gently towards the rear.

Somewhere to the north-east of Clermont Ferrand the mink decided it was feeling peckish and, tackling the nearest apparently edible object to it, began to gnaw at the insulation surrounding some of the wires of the cable loom. Its teeth didn't differentiate between plastic insulation and the wire inside. Suddenly the razor-sharp little incisors broke a fine copper strand.

It was eight minutes before John drew the captain's attention to the fact that the starboard exhaust temperature gauge was showing zero. They both attributed it to an instrument fault, and after tapping the glass a few times, ignored it.

By this time the hungry mink had decided that the insulation, despite its taste, was better than nothing and it had driven its fangs into several further wires. The starboard navigation light was now unserviceable, as was the supply to the de-icing boot on that wing.

None of these failures showed up in the cockpit, but both John and his captain ought to have noticed the amber warning light that began to glow, indicating generator failure, immediately the mink chewed through and broke the voltage-regulator relay supply cable. Perhaps if the sun hadn't been streaming in over their left shoulders and flooding the instrument panel with light, they might have seen it. But in the empty vault of the sky above the layers of fog and low cloud covering Europe, it was too brilliantly sunny for a small amber light to attract much attention.

If either pilot had looked back at the leading edge of the wing he might have been surprised to see the powerful landing-lamps flicker on and then off and on again. Or maybe one of them did, and attributed the flashes to reflections of sunlight.

The mink had bared two more wires, and as these touched, a blue flash arced across, bridging the main supply from the battery to the high wattage bulbs of the lamps.

Bereft now of all current from the generators the batteries gradually lost their charge as they supplied the essential aircraft and radio services, and dissipated their strength uselessly in illuminating the landing lights. First one generator, spinning around in time with the Hercules radial driving it, having lost voltage-regulator control, overheated and burned out. Then so did the other.

The Freighter ploughed its way serenely through the northern French sky, approaching the English Channel.

It was John who noticed first that the intercom was sounding faint, and then realised they had heard nothing on the radio for quite a while. He roused the captain. They looked for indications of a radio fault. By now the power from the battery was too weak even to make the generator-failure warning light filament glow sufficiently to be visible behind its amber glass. Even the ammeter, having tried for half-an-hour to tell them of an abnormal discharge rate, had slowly returned to its normal central position, now that there were no more amperes left to discharge.

Finally the two men realised the extent of their predicament. No electricity meant no radios, no navigation aids, not even an SBA to help them back below that billowing carpet of cloud and fog, back safely to earth. There were ninety minutes of fuel remaining, according to their flight plan, and that was all they had to go on, for fuel gauges are electric too, and all read the same: zero, zero, zero, zero.

What else was gone? The gyro-compass, the autopilot, the other engine instruments, de-icing. All they had left were their primary instruments and two steadily running, reliable radials. But exactly how long would these continue to run, and exactly where were they anyway?

Both men ran a dead-reckoning check on their present position, based on their last known fix, their course and speed since then, and an estimated wind velocity. They came up with results that were forty nautical miles apart.

After a fruitless five-minute recalculation and argument they agreed on one point. Despite the difference in calculated position, both plotted courses would lead them over the sea in less than ten minutes' time. According to the captain they would cross the French coast near Boulogne, heading towards Dover, while John's calculations put them between Gravelines and Dunkirk, heading for a long stretch of the North Sea before reaching the English coast in East Anglia.

Either way, they agreed, in ten minutes it would be safe to let right down through the overcast into the fog, to about 200 feet or even 100 feet or less if necessary, until they could see the water, then follow it towards a coast. They both put on life-jackets.

Their next trouble concerned what pressure setting to use on the altimeter. They finally agreed to turn it a few millibars higher than its Naples setting, since they vaguely remembered that pressure had been high over the UK when they had last seen a synoptic chart.

As they let down, to reach 500 feet at the time they estimated they'd be leaving the French coast, John went aft into the cargo hold to see if he could locate the electrical fault. He shone his torch to and fro, and almost immediately spotted the gleam of copper from the frayed cables. He looked aghast at the tangle. Sabotage. It couldn't be anything else. But who?

He was just about to report his suspicions when a movement caught his eye, between two of the cargo cases. The beam of his torch was reflected by two jewel-like points of light, which flickered then vanished in a flurry of fur further down towards the tail.

He had smuggled his own saboteur on board.

He returned to the right-hand seat, and reported that there was nothing to be seen except cargo.

Outside the cockpit there was nothing to be seen but cloud and mist. The altimeter crept gently anticlockwise.

1,000 feet . . . 800 feet . . . 600 feet . . . 500 . . . 400 . . . 300 . . . 200 feet.

Still nothing but clammy dampness.

Not having an accurate pressure setting meant not knowing an accurate height, and their inaccurate 200 feet could have meant very much closer to the invisible sea. But, there was no alternative. They eased the Freighter further down, to 150 feet, to 100 feet, to 80 feet, to a heart-stopping indication of 50 feet, and still the world was a dull pearly-grey sphere of mist all round, below and above.

John's mind's eye saw only one picture. The chalk cliffs of Beachy Head or Dover rushing suddenly at them from dead ahead, a shattering of aluminium and glass, of bone and sinew, then nothing . . .

There was no alternative. They had to find the surface of the earth somehow, and this was the safest place to try. They eased the Freighter slowly, slowly down until an incredible minus 40 feet showed up on the altimeter. Then the captain's nerve broke, and he put on full power, trimmed the nose up and watched their height return to a saner 1,500 feet.

They switched everything off to see if the battery would pick up enough power after a rest to work a single radio, or the SBA perhaps, for long enough to get a fix. They didn't know their landing lights were permanently shorted on.

They agreed to route from the captain's calculated position towards Ipswich, and there to let down again as low as they dared, in the hope that some turbulence over land would cause gaps in this otherwise continuous low-cloud cover. By John's calculations they'd then be flying up the middle of the North Sea, where at least there wouldn't be any square Norman church towers to pluck them from the sky.

Their second low-flying attempt was just as low, just as terrifying and just as fruitless as their first. And by the end of it neither really knew to within a hundred miles where they might be.

At least in Bomber Command they had carried parachutes.

This was bloody hopeless.

They turned east. That way they both believed lay the North Sea. Their fuel state must be getting precarious now. This time it was a let-down until they saw the surface, regardless of altimeter reading. Or until the podgy rubber tyres at the end of the Freighter's inelegant, stalky undercarriage legs hit the sea or struck something else.

Flying steadily east they reached minus 40 feet again, still without seeing a thing. Then two things happened simultaneously. John thought he saw a faint gleam of light ahead of him, and the starboard engine cut suddenly, banged once and died. The captain struggled to control the asymmetric forces but dropped the starboard wing. One wheel hit a wave; they lurched starboard and the wing-tip struck the water.

Pieces of the aircraft began to break off, and what was left of it cartwheeled once in a flurry of spray before coming to a juddering halt in the sea.

John struggled out of his seat. He saw in a single shocked glance that his captain, with the control column embedded into his chest, was beyond any hope of rescue. He grabbed the escape axe from the bulkhead to smash his way out of the cockpit. Just as the hulk of the Freighter, minus most of its starboard wing, slipped below the water, John squeezed through the shattered perspex and hit the icy waters of the North Sea. He flipped the toggle on his life-jacket and the gas rushed from the cylinder to inflate it, holding him under the armpits and keeping his head clear of the sluggish swell.

Then he saw the yellow glow again. It must be one of the lightships in the Channel, he thought. All he had to do now was swim towards it, and he'd save his skin. Poor swimmer that he was, he thanked God for inflatable life-jackets. John began to believe he could distinguish the silhouette of a ship below the patch of light. Not much further.

Then he saw something else. Brown and furry, with the brightest imaginable pair of dark eyes sparkling at him, the escaped mink was swimming towards him, looking out of place, yet quite at home in the water.

He stopped swimming and let it approach him. It came towards him from the side, and as it did it sank its claws and teeth into the yellow fabric of the life-jacket. There was a hiss and gurgle as the carbon dioxide bubbled out and the jacket flapped uselessly around John's face. He tried vainly to dog-paddle, to keep his face clear of the water, to yell for help. Only a few weak gurgling noises came, too faint for anyone to hear, before he finally slipped beneath the chill waters.

The mink swam efficiently and purposefully towards the Norfolk coast near Sheringham only a few hundred yards away. It scuttled across the sands shaking the water from its fur and startling a cluster of black-headed gulls on the shore into a frenzy of squawking. Then it scampered easily up the zig-zag path that cut through the tall sandy cliffs. It followed the path through a tangle of brilliant yellow gorse bushes and past the cottage at the top, then headed off into the freedom of the gentle green countryside of East Anglia.

Chapter 14
DOWN IN THE GLEN

Whenever conversation turns to the subject of the merits and demerits of flying clubs, my thoughts return to that best-of-all 'clubs' of which I once had the good fortune to be a member . . . a University Air Squadron.

After World War II these units were being re-created in an unsophisticated and ever so slightly disorganised way. The instructors all had seen active service; their medal ribbons bore witness to experiences over the Western Desert, Burma and the Normandy beaches, to long, dark Lancaster sorties or to lonely North Atlantic convoy vigils in Sunderlands. Some of the squadron members were ex-RAF or FAA pilots, too, but most of us were ex-schoolboy undergraduates starry-eyed if slightly overawed by our learned and experienced mentors and fellow members.

We were, in general, impecunious. Student grants in those days weren't even what they are now. To be paid in hard coin of the realm for each hour we flew, for every evening of ground school, was a scarcely credible by-product of membership. At least it helped us afford to learn how to sink pint for pint with our more mature colleagues at the Squadron bar on Saturday evenings.

Flying training was strict, well disciplined and based on the RAF curriculum. In those days, one could remain a member throughout one's university course, for three or four years or even longer, and as a result some cadets amassed amazing totals of hours of *ab initio* Tiger Moth time. The dual hours logged tended by comparison to be a trifle unbalanced. Our instructors were more accustomed to the comparative luxury of the cockpits of Mosquitos or Mustangs, Marylands or even Meteors, than the spartan joys of Magisters and Tiger Moths, so they preferred the quick up and down of an aerobatic or spinning exercise to the long, cold drag of a cross-country at 80 knots through wintry Scottish skies. As a result our dual training was long on slow rolls and short on long sorties of a navigational nature.

However, the sadists used to make sure we got plenty of the latter in the form of solo cross-countries. The instructors generally were interested enough to check, before we left the comfort of the crew-room, that we hadn't drawn our triangles of velocity with the wind in the wrong direction. But thereafter we were on our own.

For our part, we generally managed to identify at least some of the turning points, and we usually managed to find our way back to base without untoward incident.

Usually, but not always.

From time to time our flying scenery was varied from that surrounding our home base, when we went to 'camp' at another airfield, or on attachment to another UAS or RFS (Reserve Flying School).

In my case, home was a soggy field with steel mesh tracking runways which did not agree at all with Tiger Moth tail skids. Then it was known as Royal Naval Air Station *HMS Sanderling*. Now it is Glasgow's impressive Abbotsinch Airport. It wasn't long before I acquired a thorough knowledge of the Firth of Clyde and Loch Lomond from the rear cockpit of Glasgow UAS's Magisters.

Then we 'converted' to Tigers at Perth, and I began to familiarise myself with a Moth's eye view of the Central Highlands. At camps, we mingled our circuits with those of B-29s at Waddington and learned to love the expansive landscapes of Lincolnshire and East Anglia. From Ouston I navigated my way around the hills of Northumbria, marvelling at the architecture of Hadrian's Wall as seen from the air. From Fairoaks I learned how to cope with the 'busy' traffic of south-east England, while Heathrow was just a colossal muddy construction site, and Hendon a much busier airfield than Gatwick.

Control zones? Never heard of them.

VHF radios? What good would one of these be? Every airfield had a signals square, hadn't it?

These were the halcyon days before we had to trade our open cockpits, Gosport tubes and Sidcot suits for the hyper-modernity of the Chipmunk with its greenhouse comfort and the curse of a VHF set.

During one of our periods away from base, at Perth aerodrome one autumn weekend, I was detailed to carry out a cross-country with a purpose. One of the Aberdeen UAS Tigers had just completed a major in the workshops at Perth and was due to be ferried back to Dyce. Another, its hours almost used up, was to be ferried back to Perth for servicing. My job was to act as ferry pilot, with the bonus that I could use up the final four hours flying time before the major was due on the second Tiger, by way of a free-lance cross-country on my way back. I flight-planned for a quick look at John-o'-Groats, refuelling at Dalcross near Inverness.

'If this stuff doesn't break up before you leave Dyce', said 'Hutch', my W/O instructor, looking at the seven oktas hanging around 1,500 feet that morning, 'you'd better do your John-o'-Groats trip along the coast past Wick, and never mind navigating through the mountains.' I agreed quite happily. With no radio and no radar around, exactly where pupils went on nav-exercises was always something of a mystery to instructors. (If they knew where the cadets current heart-throb lived, they could often have gone there and disproved logs that claimed the aircraft was straight and level at one place, while actually being observed executing inexpert aerobatics overhead the girl-friend's home. But that would have been unethical.)

The 'Form 700' (airframe and engine logs) mustn't ever fly in the aircraft they refer to. So a second DH82A was going to Dyce from Perth that day, too, to carry the sets of paperwork in both directions. Johnny was detailed to take off fifteen minutes ahead of me. There was to be no nonsense about formation flying up to Dyce; we hadn't covered that part of the syllabus yet.

The newly-serviced Tiger started easily, and climbed briskly off Perth's smooth grass. I followed the take-off track Johnny had used a quarter of an hour earlier, the grass duller where his slipstream had blown away the morning dew.

It wasn't really all that much of a surprise to me when, just after flying over Glamis Castle, keeping about 500 feet below cloud-base, I was suddenly buzzed by another Tiger Moth. Johnny, who had been circling in or near the cloud-base was practising a three-quarter beam attack from above and astern. He zipped across, just above me, pulled parallel to me on the port side and, as he overtook me, entered a nicely executed barrel roll, then waved me in to join him.

We flew in company over Forfar and Brechin. Johnny was leader, kept beckoning me into closer formation, and laughing, as if to call me 'chicken' every time I decided I was close enough already. Then by hand signals he indicated he was abdicating, and I was to be leader. In echelon starboard Johnny showed me just how close two Moths could fly.

Near Inverbervie we reached the coast and clear blue skies simultaneously. I indicated 'up', opened the throttle and the two Tigers clawed their way up to around 3,000 feet. Now I was playing 'chicken', as I pulled into a steep turn. Johnny stayed with me. He even manoeuvred from starboard to port echelon between two of my turns, and finally, as I gritted my teeth, he held position, his wing-tip tucked in behind mine right round a loop.

Grinning like a Cheshire cat, Johnny waved *au revoir* and dived off ahead of me over Stonehaven, heading for Dyce.

If poor Johnny hadn't died in a test flying accident at Farnborough a few years later, he surely would have made it into one of the RAF teams that preceded the Red Arrows.

For my part I loitered awhile in the sunshine above the fishing harbour at Stonehaven, then pottered quietly north along the coastline to overfly the Granite City in a lazy circle, before landing at Dyce. It was only politic to leave a decent interval between Johnny's landing and my own arrival.

'Good flight?' he asked me in the Aberdeen UAS hut.

'Not bad', I told him. 'And you?'

Johnny swapped the paperwork and headed back for Perth. I swapped aircraft and by about ten o'clock was winging my way towards the north-west, under conditions we know today as CAVOK.

With occasional glances at the big compass down between my knees and much more attention to the lovely countryside below me, I watched some of the names I only knew from malt whisky labels embody themselves as villages and distilleries nestling among the purple hills. Tomintoul, Knockandhu and Tomnavoulin in the famous Glen of the River Livet all passed below me as did Dufftown and Longmorn. Then I decided I'd better keep well south of the naval and air force stations at Lossiemouth and Kinloss, and head straight for Dalcross, to land and refuel.

The little float fuel gauge didn't seem to have moved very far, but the corrugated tank in the mid-section of the upper wing absorbed about eight gallons, which I signed for quite happily. His Majesty would foot the bill. After a couple of swings the Gipsy Major coughed into life again, and I headed north over Fort George and the Moray Firth, over the Black Isle to the Cromarty Firth then over the hills of Easter Ross to the Dornoch Firth.

The few clouds that were around were too high to worry me. I was exploring a part of my native land I'd never seen before, and I had no wish to climb any farther than I had to in order to clear the hills. I wanted to see the countryside, to scent the whiff of bracken burning on the flanks of Beinn Tharsuinn, to smell the characteristic peaty aroma of a Scottish moor. And that's something you can't do very effectively in a modern spam-cam.

My flight-planned route was almost due magnetic north across the wilderness of hills that forms most of the County of Sutherland, to meet the Atlantic Ocean near Tongue on the north coast of Scotland, then along the coast east to John-o'-Groats. From there it was to be an easy coast crawl back to refuel at Dalcross again before turning the Tiger Moth over to the maintenance men at Perth, its airworthy hours nicely used up.

All went well until, about half-an-hour out of Dalcross, flying over Tain at the south end of Loch Shin I thought I felt an odd vibration in the old girl's frame. It went away again, and a glance around the rather meagre engine instrumentation revealed nothing amiss. So I pressed on.

Near the lonely inn perched in the empty hills at Altnaharra the Tiger gave another tremor. This time it was quite distinct, and quite persistent. I tried various throttle settings. None of them helped, so at full chat I gained a bit of height above the hills. I reasoned it might just come in handy.

From the map, with its sea of purple hypsometric tinting, it looked as though my nearest airfield wasn't Dalcross any more. If I had time to get there, Thurso or Wick would be closer. So I pressed on, up and north. Then the vibration became alarming at full throttle, so I eased off the power and trimmed for level flight. I reached out the cockpit with my left hand and flicked down each of the magneto switches in turn. One didn't seem to make much difference, but the other caused the vibration to increase quite drastically.

The Gipsy was sick, and getting gradually sicker. I looked below. The landscape was inhospitable, and didn't look like getting any less so. Barren hills, steep glens, everywhere I looked. And not a sign of habitation. I followed the only road in sight, farther and farther north. The vibrations developed into distinct judders, and I remembered instructions about 'precautionary' landings (now called 'forced landings with power') and how these were preferable to genuine forced landings once all power had gone.

I decided that the next level-looking bit of ground would have to do duty as a temporary aerodrome. None of it looked very level until right at the southern end of Loch Loyal there appeared a cottage beside the empty road, and a fairly flat-looking little field behind it.

Power eased back, the Gipsy still banged and spluttered a bit as I flew across the field, a hundred feet or so above the cottage.

A man emerged, peering curiously at me, his hand shading his eyes. At least there was someone down there. The field looked acceptable for landing, so with a glance at the peat smoke from the chimney of the croft I assessed the wind velocity then opened up the throttle. I got to about 500 feet before I decided the engine was going to blow herself up unless I reduced power, so I completed an erratic low circuit over the silvery, rippled water of the loch, lined up and landed. The surface was firm, but bumpy. The Tiger's tail skid dug in as I held the stick well back, and I didn't even feel the need for brakes as she stopped in about half the length of the field. I glanced across at the cottage. The man was now studying me carefully through a telescope. Feeling decidedly self-conscious I gingerly gave a trickle of power, very rough and un-Gipsy-like power, taxied over close to the croft, and turned the sorry-sounding engine off.

My ears were singing in the silence as I slipped off my helmet. I unlatched the cockpit door, stepped clumsily on to the ground in my sheepskin-lined flying boots and went across towards the old man with the telescope. As I approached it was he who broke the silence.

'Iss there something the matter with your airy-o-plane?' he asked, seriously, in the lilting English accent of a native Gaelic speaker.

Biting my tongue, I refrained from the sarcastic reply.

'There's something up with the engine. Running rough', I explained.

'It wass sounding even worrse than my Son's motor-picycle', he informed me.

I asked if I might telephone the police or even Perth perhaps. He smiled gently and told me the nearest telephone line was in Tongue, more than ten miles away over the mountain roads. I suggested I might get a lift to there. He smiled again.

'It issn't much traffic that we're getting over this road now the towrists are away home. Yesterday wass the day for the postie, and the baker issn't due till Thursday.'

I looked at him, unbelieving. But he was quite serious. I looked at the road, miles of it in both directions. Empty. And I remembered all the way I'd flown over it from Altnaharra Inn I hadn't noticed a single vehicle of any sort.

'What about your son's motor bike?'

'He iss away on it, in the hills, with the sheep', he told me, raising his telescope again, and sweeping it slowly along the mountain-fringed horizon. 'He iss still on the other side, so he'll not be back till chust before sunset, I am thinking. It iss a pity too', he added, 'for it iss he who iss knowing about motors and things and could maybe chust help you mend your airy-o-plane motor too.'

The idea of effecting a repair hadn't occurred to me, even though my university subject was mechanical engineering. For a moment I brightened, then realised that without tools I might as well have been a divinity student. In fact, a divinity student might well have been better equipped for this situation than I.

'There iss some tools and things in the shed behind the croft', the old man said, as if reading my mind, and led me round to view them. Rusty spanners, broken valve springs, the bent half-shaft from a truck, a clutch plate from a motor bicycle, some chains, a box of nuts and bolts, and sundry screwdrivers lay jumbled together around a workbench with a vice.

The trouble, I decided, could just possibly be no more than fouled plugs, and if so, with the help of some of this junk, I could maybe fix it. At least it would be better than doing nothing, and much better than walking ten mountain miles in sheepskin flying boots.

At this juncture another person appeared. She and the man started speaking rapidly in Gaelic, casting the odd suspicious look in my direction. I chose a brief lull in the conversation to air one of the few phrases of Gaelic I knew.

'*Ciamar a tha thu?*' I ventured. How do you do?

The suspicious look vanished from the woman's face as she gave the spontaneous answer '*Tha mi gle mhath*', and added, 'So it issn't a Sassenach you are then?'

Moments later their son's comprehensive tool-kit, including a plug spanner, was out of its cupboard, and I was invited to lunch.

'It iss but a humble home we are haffing, but we would be honoured to haff you share a bittie meat with us.'

Some fiddling with spanners and tommy bars, some scraped knuckles and oily fingernails soon saw the sparking plugs out of the engine. Several of them had their electrodes shrouded with lead and black carbon deposits. Maybe I could effect a cure after all?

The old boy and I sat in the sunshine on the doorstep of the croft with my penknife, his baccy knife and his wife's scouring pad, and we picked and scraped and polished away at the plugs. Mrs McLeod, for we'd learned each other's names by now, brought the broth to the boil and heated up a mutton stew, which may have been humble, but was also delicious.

The gleaming plugs went back into place without mishap; the engine was soon cowled up again, after a deft tap on the impulse magneto to ensure it didn't stick. I dumped boulders in front of each tyre as chocks and explained to Mr McLeod how to operate the switches and throttle, and how to hold the front cockpit stick back. He was a fast learner for an elderly man. The engine caught on the second swing.

I climbed into the rear cockpit while Mr McLeod kept the Gipsy ticking over at idling revs. He sat there quite happily, his grey hair whipping about in the slipstream as I warmed up the engine and checked the mag drop. She was running as sweet as a nut again. I throttled back, leaned forward and yelled to the old man. '*Is mah sin!* It's okay now . . . Time to go.' He clambered awkwardly out of the cockpit and down the walkway in the slipstream.

'Watch out for the propeller when you move the stones away', I warned him.

'I'll be toing chust that, too', he shouted back. 'And would you be so good ass to send uss a post-card, chust to let uss know it iss home safely that you are?'

The take-off was very bouncy, but safe. I circled low over the croft. She was waving a tea-towel; he was peering through his telescope again; of the son, or the sheep or the motor bike there was still no sign.

I made sure at Dalcross that the fuel I got was 83 octane and not 100/130, for I still suspect that may have been the cause of my failing to see John-o'-Groats. Back in Perth 'Hutch' was in too much of a hurry to get off into town to do more than a cursory debriefing or to query my somewhat tardy return to base.

'Enjoy the trip?'

'Yes, it was fine up to . . .'

'Aircraft okay?'

'Was running a bit rough, but . . .'

'It's due a major anyway, so that's not surprising. See you in the morning.' And he was off.

I decided that since I'd broken several RAF rules, written or unwritten, I'd maybe better not press the point. The intention was in my mind to tell Johnny all about my adventure that night, but at the party in the RAFVR club we were both so busy trying to steal each other's girls, there just wasn't a suitable opportunity. (Good friend as he was, Johnny eventually did get my girl. I was present later at their nuptials in Nottingham . . . and later mourned with her at his funeral in Farnborough.)

So the incident of the Tiger in the field beside the lonely croft at the south end of Loch Loyal never did get aired. I sent the McLeods a little more than a p.c. The postie on his journey the following Monday should have delivered a woollen scarf in the appropriate tartan for her, and four ounces (which was more than I could really afford) of the tobacco I'd noticed he smoked, for him.

That was the end of the incident . . . at least until many years later. I was in the RAF by then, stationed back in Scotland, at Kinloss. It was the bitter winter of 1957/58 and most of Scotland lay buried under mountainous snowdrifts. In January 1958 the Automobile Association's DH 89A Dragon Rapide was operating out of various Scottish highland airfields where strenuous efforts had kept the runways clear. Its pilot, Bill Lewis with his magnificent handlebar moustache, was busy trying to locate motorists stranded amidst the snowdrifts, and dropping food packs to them.

Perhaps inspired by the AA's example, our Station Commander, Group Captain Thompson, brought into being 'Operation Snowdrop'. Bales of hay, bags of foodstuffs, sacks of cattle cake and sheep fodder were collected from the rich farmlands of Morayshire, loaded into Neptunes and Shackletons and dropped to starving animals in the mountains, and to isolated hamlets, cut off for days. I flew on some of these trips, and on one I spotted the outline of Ben Loyal over on the horizon. It rang a little bell in my memory.

'Let's take a look over there', I said to the captain. 'There's an isolated croft down at the south end of the Loch, and maybe they could be doing with some supplies.'

The huge bulk of the Shackleton thundered down the length of Loch Loyal and roared over the roof of the tiny building.

'Nobody there', was the comment. 'Bloody place looks uninhabited', but none the less we swung round for a second look. And suddenly there they were. Three figures, one waving a tea-towel, the other peering through a telescope, and a third one running, hands outstretched, through the snow, a dog beside him. The road to Tongue was invisible, totally obliterated by snow.

I squeezed back to the open doors of the aircraft. Over the din of the contra-rotating props and the shriek of the slipstream I yelled, 'A couple of bales of sheep stuff and some iron rations here.' Moments later the airmen acting as 'bomb aimers' had sent several packages plummeting earthwards. They landed close enough. The last thing I saw was the man with the dog beginning to haul one back towards the croft.

'Have this lunch on me', I murmured to myself as we swung to starboard, heading out towards our official target area nearer Cape Wrath.

Not for a moment do I imagine these gentle folk would ever associate that monstrous noisy Shackleton bringing them succour from the skies with the youngster in the sick Tiger Moth who had visited them a decade earlier.

Nor have I ever been back to explain the connection.